W9-CEO-652

THE HOUSE OF SIXTY FATHERS

Other books by Meindert DeJong . . .

BILLY AND THE UNHAPPY BULL

THE CAT THAT WALKED A WEEK

DIRK'S DOG BELLO

GOOD LUCK DUCK

HURRY HOME, CANDY

THE LITTLE COW AND THE TURTLE

THE LITTLE STRAY DOG

SHADRACH

SMOKE ABOVE THE LANE

THE TOWER BY THE SEA

THE WHEEL ON THE SCHOOL

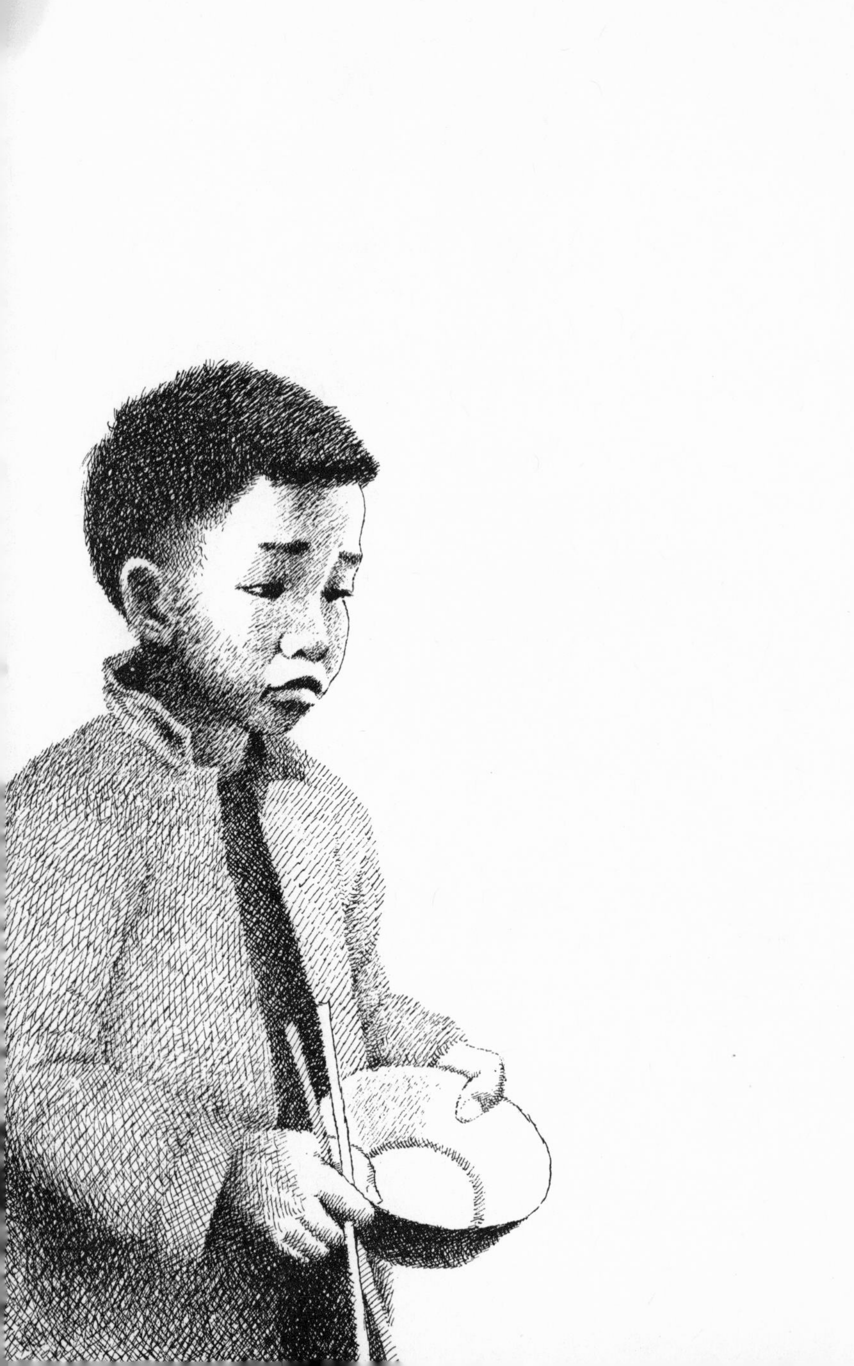

THE HOUSE OF SIXTY FATHERS

by MEINDERT DEJONG

Author of THE WHEEL ON THE SCHOOL, winner of the *John Newbery Award*

pictures by MAURICE SENDAK

HARPER & ROW, PUBLISHERS, NEW YORK AND EVANSTON

THE HOUSE OF SIXTY FATHERS

Printed in the United States of America

Library of Congress catalog card number: 56-8148

For Wally

in memory of the compound in Peishiyi, China,

and of little, lost Panza

CONTENTS

THE HOUSE OF SIXTY FATHERS

CHAPTER ONE

RAIN ON THE SAMPAN

Rain raised the river. Rain beat down on the sampan where it lay in a long row of sampans tied to the riverbank. Rain drummed down on the mats that were shaped in the form of an arched roof over the middle of the sampan. It clattered hard on the four long oars lying on top of the roof of mats.

The rain found the bullethole in the roof of mats. Thick drops of water dripped through the bullethole onto the neck of the family pig, sleeping on the floor of the sampan. The little pig twitched his neck every time a big, cold drop of water hit it, but he went on sleeping.

Tien Pao looked on in quiet amusement to see how many cold drops it would take to wake the pig. It took nine—then with a disgusted grunt the little pig slid over just far enough to get his neck from under the drip.

But the drip from the bullethole began making a big puddle on the floor. With his bare toes Tien Pao shoved the dishpan with the three ducklings under the drip. He settled himself on the bench again, and leaned his head against the wall of mats.

The little pig was sound asleep. The ducklings went to sleep in a little huddle at the bottom of the dishpan. The drumming of the rain on the matting overhead became so monotonous, Tien Pao's head began to nod. Under half-shut eyelids he saw the sleeping ducklings rise on the water that dripped into their pan. They drifted in their sleep. The big, monotonous drops kept stirring the water.

Rain raised the river. The sampan swayed and bobbed on the rising water. Voices drifted from the other sampans in the long row of sampans and muttered among the drumming rain. Tien Pao closed his eyes and almost slept, and yet he didn't sleep. He sat sagged against the mats, dreamily remembering the hard days just past, the hard journey.

It had been a long journey. Tien Pao had lost count of all the days and nights. But all those nights when the horns of the new moon had stood dimly in the sky, Tien Pao and his father and mother had pushed the sampan on and on against the currents of the endless rivers. Day and night. There was no stopping even at night. "We won't stop until we drop," Tien Pao's father had kept saying over and over. "And we won't drop until we are far inside this great land of China. Far from the sea—for where the sea is, there the Japanese invaders are."

The family pig, the three ducklings, and the little stone mill to grind the rice for the baby sister—these they had saved from the mud house of the family of Tien that had stood a little beyond their village of The-Corner-of-the-Mountains-Where-the-Rivers-Meet. Besides these they had saved absolutely nothing, except Beauty-of-the-Republic, Tien Pao's baby sister.

Suddenly one morning the Japanese had come. Bullets had whined through the crooked streets of the village, bullets had pierced the mud walls of the houses, people had screamed. There had been terrible screams inside the houses.

The Japanese soldiers had come in at one end of the village, and like a herd of lowing cattle the villagers had run out of the other end—to the river and the sampans. They had crowded into the sampans, they had shoved them madly into the river.

Over the river had come a snarling roar. Japanese planes had burst out of the clouds, had hurtled themselves at the crowded sampans. Bullets had stuttered out of the screeching, diving planes, a horrible hail of bullets had slammed into the sampans.

Back and back the planes had come with their hail of bullets, while sampans sank and went under. Back and back until there was but one empty sampan left drifting on the water. Then the planes had come no more—not for one empty sampan. It had drifted silently—empty.

The family of Tien had seen it all from the clump of bamboos at the edge of the river where they had crouched. The planes had passed, the air above the river was still and empty, but now the shooting in the village had drawn nearer. "Now! Now!" Tien Hsu, the father, had whispered in the bamboo clump to his little family. "It is now, or never." He had plunged into the river after the drifting sampan. Tien Pao and his mother, with Beauty-of-the-Republic strapped to her back, had plunged after him. His mother had the rice mill, Tien Pao had the family pig under one arm, the dishpan with the ducklings squeezed against his chest. But his father had boarded the empty sampan, and his father had pulled everything and everybody on board. He had simply pulled Tien Pao up by his head and his neck, while Tien Pao clung to the pig and the dishpan.

Then Tien Pao's father had run to the back of the sampan and had grabbed the oars. Tien Pao had started for the front of the sampan to take the oars there. But his mother had caught him and flung him to the floor of the sampan. "No!" she'd whispered fiercely. "Children must live." She'd unstrapped the baby and had pushed her at Tien Pao where he lay on the floor; she'd made Tien Pao hold his hand over the hole made by a Japanese bullet in the floor of the sampan, and she had gone to the oars at the front of the sampan.

On the floor Tien Pao had held Beauty-of-the-Republic tightly against him, while with his other hand he'd twisted his cap into a prop to shove into the bullethole through which the river water came welling. He had lain on the prop to keep the water from pushing it out again, and he'd lain half over

the baby sister to shield her if the airplanes and the bullets should come again.

His father and his mother had stood upright at the oars. And no bullets had come, no airplanes had hurtled at them out of the clouds.

But behind him Tien Pao had heard the roar of the flames as the whole village burned. The flames in a great hungry sweep had rushed from thatched roof to thatched roof, and the hollow bamboo framework inside the mud walls had exploded with the terrifying sound of guns. Sparks had rained on the river from the explosions, and the sampan had swept on in water gone red from the flames.

In the leaping, sharp brightness of the flames Tien Pao's mother and father stood upright. Stern and silent at the great oars, they had pushed the sampan up the river away from the sparks and explosions of the roaring village.

The sampan had gone up many rivers in the following days and nights. Out of great rivers—as rivers grow great as they near the sea—into smaller, narrowing rivers the farther they went inland. Push and pull, and pull and push at the long sweeping oars, day and night. Night and day, always against the current. Tien Pao had taken his turn at the oars for long, hard hours, spelling his father or his mother by night or by day in the endless hard journey.

Now at last the sampan lay tied to the bank at the end of a long row of sampans that belonged at this river town of Hengyang. This was Tien Pao's first whole day of rest.

Tien Pao's father and mother had not rested. The family of Tien was now safe from the Japanese, but they were penniless in a strange, big city. There was no food in the sampan. They had the sampan and nothing else—they must find work immediately, or starve.

Last night the Hengyang river people on the other sampans had told them that there was much work at a great field for airplanes not many miles from the town. This morning, in the early, dark, rainy dawn, Tien Pao's father and his mother, with the baby strapped to her back, had gone with their new neighbors. Now it was late afternoon, and they had not come back. It must mean that they were working for the white foreigners—the American airmen, who had come over the ocean from a strange, far land to help the Chinese fight the Japanese invaders.

Tien Pao had not understood it too well when last night the new neighbors had explained about the great airfield to his father—he'd been too stupefied with weariness. He had not known that airplanes needed fields, almost as if they were cows or grazing goats. He had never seen a white foreigner.

But airplanes he knew! Airplanes came screaming out of the sky, and out of them bullets stuttered, and then water spat, and sampans sank, and people fell, and a whole village burned while in an empty river red from flames one sampan drifted on red water.

Tien Pao moaned aloud. His own moan roused him. He jumped to his feet and stood shivering. He shook himself to get rid of the evil memories. It was rain dark inside the sampan. And the dark was scary; he was scared. He hurried to the saucer of oil that stood before the mirror in the little altar to the river god, and tremblingly lit the wick. The flickering, smoking saucer lamp reflected in the altar mirror and sent yellow rays of light over the ducklings and the pig.

Tien Pao looked at them, and not at the wedge of wood that had been driven into the sampan floor to close the hole made by the Japanese bullet. And his lips mumbled—grateful for the light. "The light is good, and the river god that sent us the sampan is good," he whispered. But he couldn't help the last little shiver that still ran through him as he bowed and bowed himself before the altar of the good river god who had sent the sampan and had saved the whole family of Tien.

Outside all at once the other sampans became noisy with shouts. The rain must have stopped.

For a moment the sinking evening sun shone briefly bright over the river. Women and children from all the sampans were swarming up the riverbank, outshouting each other to attract the attention of some passenger who wanted to be ferried across the river. Tien Pao peered through a crack in the mats, but he couldn't see the top of the bank. He pushed the mat aside and stepped out. But when he looked up the high bank, he had to cling to the matting for support. On top of the riverbank stood the river god!

It must be the river god! His hair was golden, and his face was white. In that white face were pale-blue eyes. People had dark hair, dark eyes! It must be the river god!

At that moment the god on top of the riverbank looked right at Tien Pao. And then he came plunging down the high bank straight toward Tien Pao and the narrow gangplank that reached from the sampan to the shore. Tien Pao clutched the matting. "Mother!" he croaked.

He could stand there no longer. He dived into the sampan, shoved the mats across the opening. He looked wildly about him. He grabbed the sleeping pig—the family pig was the best thing he had, he'd offer the pig to the river god. He dashed with the little pig to the far end of the sampan and stood trembling before the river god's own altar.

The mats parted. The golden-haired, blue-eyed god stepped into the sampan. Tien Pao's knees quaked under him, but somehow he managed to take a few steps forward. He almost shoved the little pig into the white one's arms. Then he backed away to the altar again, bowing deeply to the god as he backed toward the god's own altar.

The strange white one stood in the opening looking in open-mouthed surprise from the little pig that had been tossed into his arms to the bowing, scraping Tien Pao. Suddenly he threw his head back and out of him came a great howling roar of laughter. The god laughed!

It was too much for Tien Pao. In his confusion he desperately dashed past the roaring river god and out of the sampan. The new neighbor woman was still standing outside her sampan. "Please, please, I don't know what the strange white river god wants of me," Tien Pao managed to whisper.

The woman, too, laughed at him. "Stranger child, he is not a god. He is an American airman from the great field for airplanes. And he wants you to take him over the river. He picked you, I guess, because you did not shout his ears off like the rest of us."

"Oh," Tien Pao said. He felt foolish and small. And he'd given the family pig to the airman, who was only a foreigner. "Oh, but I may not ferry people across the river," Tien Pao told the woman doubtfully. "My father forbade me ever to take the sampan away from the bank."

"Oh, but you must take the airman," the woman said. "This is different. You will see, he will pay you much yen. Why, he may even pay you as much as one hundred yen, when he should only pay ten. And, from what I heard, your father and mother could use the money."

One hundred yen! Tien Pao looked back at the sampan. A hundred yen just for going across the river—money for food. If his father and mother hadn't found work . . . Why, for a hundred yen his father would know he'd just *had* to take the sampan away from the bank!

Tien Pao hesitated no longer. He pulled down two of the long oars. He loosed the rope from the stout stake driven into the bank, and pulled in the gangplank. He shoved the sampan into the river. The next moment the river grabbed the sampan. The rain-swollen current was swift and savage. Tien Pao struggled, but from the first it was a losing fight. The nose of the boat swirled around, the sampan swung and raced downstream. Tien Pao fought, but he was weak—he'd had no food all day, and almost none yesterday and the day before. In spite of him, the boat swept on downstream.

Inside the sampan the white stranger must have become alarmed. He came running outside. He looked at the racing river, at Tien Pao struggling with the big oars. He seemed to take in the situation at once, for he hauled down the second set of oars, gave Tien Pao a big encouraging grin, and strode to the front of the sampan with the oars.

It went better at once, much better. Soon they began holding their own, and then they were cleaving the current in a long, sweeping arc toward the opposite shore. Much sooner than Tien Pao at the back of the boat had expected, the sampan thumped the bank across the river.

The soldier came back to place the oars on the roof of mats. He and Tien Pao grinned at each other. The soldier fished in his pocket, brought up a hundred-yen note, and handed it to Tien Pao —as if it were so much wrapping paper!

"It is too much, too much," Tien Pao said in consternation. "Why, you rowed yourself across, and I should have no pay at all."

Of course, the soldier could not understand. He evidently did not know even a single Chinese word. He just grinned and shook his head when Tien Pao shoved the hundred-yen note back at him. Then, without waiting for the gangplank, he took a running jump to the shore. He disappeared in the evening shadows gathering under the high riverbank. And he had not taken the little pig!

"I'll wait for you," Tien Pao eagerly shouted after him. "I'll take you back, and you won't have to pay one yen. Not even one little yen!"

Tien Pao peered into the dark again. The riverbank loomed black in the gathering night. Still the white soldier did not come. Tien Pao fingered the hundred-yen note again for a little reassurance. He was anxious. Night had come. The rain had started again. By now his father and mother with the baby sister must be back from the field for airplanes, and there'd be no sampan at the riverbank.

What if the foreign soldier didn't come back! He couldn't take the sampan across the dark river alone.

The saucer lamp before the altar guttered out. The last oil was gone. In the pitch dark of the sampan Tien Pao felt his way to the altar and prayed to the river god before the dark altar. "God, give me strength. Give me strength." He'd have to try it. He didn't dare wait any longer—they'd be waiting for him on the riverbank. But wait until they saw the hundred-yen note, then his father wouldn't be so angry. A hundred yen! "God, give me strength." If only he weren't so hungry . . .

Oh, they'd be scared—the sampan gone. Tien Pao clenched his lips and dug an oar into the mud to free the sampan from the bank. But the river god must have heard him, for before the boat could move away from the bank into the current, a light came plunging down the steep bank. The long beam searched the riverside, found the sampan, picked out Tien Pao at the oars, and then the airman's foreign voice shouted things at him. Tien Pao almost wept for joy.

The airman's voice sounded glad, too. He jumped on board. Now he hauled down the oars and hurried to the front of the sampan. They pushed off. The sampan swung into the current.

In the total dark the river seemed even more violent and treacherous than when they had first crossed it. The rushing sound of the river was all around them, but the white soldier in the front shouted above it. He kept up his meaningless but encouraging shouts all the way.

Now and then his powerful light would flash and search the river, and Tien Pao would see his big, easy, reassuring grin. Tien Pao used every bit of his strength. The boat forged ahead, but, anxious as he was, the crossing seemed endless to Tien Pao.

Then suddenly they were landing. Tien Pao had not seen the bank at all. The rain beat in his face and blinded and confused him. They were landing, but they were landing clumsily. They crashed so hard into the end sampan of the long row of sampans that the whole boat shuddered. The soldier's light flashed briefly.

At that anxious busy moment Tien Pao heard a desperate call through the dark and rain. "Tien Pao?" It was his mother calling the piteous question from the top of the high bank.

Tien Pao fought the huge, clumsy oars to make the boat slide ahead into its proper slot. There was no time to answer.

"Tien Pao?" Misery was in his mother's scared call.

Tien Pao opened his mouth as if to answer, but his voice strangled in his throat. It took all his wits, all his strength, and all his attention now to keep the boat from being swept downriver again. The soldier shouted something.

"Tien Pao?" And now his mother must be plunging straight down the steep, slippery bank. Her voice seemed to come plunging. She was crying.

At that moment the soldier in the front dug his oar into the river-bottom mud. The sampan shot ahead with such force it slid partly up the mud flat underneath the bank. It lay solid. They had landed!

"MOTHER!" Tien Pao shouted. She must be picking her way down the slippery bank, maybe she'd fallen in the dark. Now she wasn't answering.

Instead, a paper lantern came swinging wildly along the flats below the bank. It was Tien Pao's father. He came toward the sampan in big, running strides. He set down the lantern. He shouldered the white soldier aside and stood over Tien Pao. Without a word he held out his hand for the oars. He turned and took the soldier's two oars. "A son of mine who breaks his word I will no longer trust—ever," he said in stiff, hard words to the soldier. He did not speak to Tien Pao.

But then Tien Pao's mother at last was there. By the light of the paper lantern Tien Pao saw that she was soaked through and through. Even the baby sister on her back was soaked, the coolie hat had not been enough shelter and protection. And his mother's trousers and jacket were covered with mud—she had fallen.

Tien Pao stood mute, the hundred-yen note

squeezed in his hand. The soldier looked at him, looked at Tien Pao's crying mother. Nobody said a word. The soldier fished awkwardly in his pocket. He came up with another hundred-yen note. He thrust it into Tien Pao's hand, and he patted Tien Pao on the head so Tien Pao's mother would see.

Tien Pao's mother picked up the paper lantern and went into the sampan. The soldier, with a helpless shrug and a look at Tien Pao, turned, and then he was gone in the night. Tien Pao hurried after his mother.

Inside the sampan Tien Pao's mother was unstrapping the baby sister, but when she looked at the soaked baby, her face worked. She stripped the wet clothes off the baby, held her out to Tien Pao to hold while she rummaged in a chest under the bench for something dry.

With his mother kneeling before the chest, her back to him, it was easier to explain. "A hundred yen for taking the foreign airman across, and a hundred yen for taking him back!" Tien Pao said loudly to make it sound as impressive as possible. "And, Mother, the neighbor woman said I had to take him across. And I thought—suppose you and father hadn't found work, and there I'd have two hundred yen!"

His mother said nothing.

Tien Pao refused to be silenced by her silence.

"Two hundred yen for a little trip across and back," he said stubbornly.

His mother took the baby from him and wrapped it in a square of dry cloth. "Sit down with her, and turn your back, while I take off these drenched clothes."

Over the sleeping baby sister Tien Pao earnestly explained everything all over again to his mother. Then before he knew it he was blurting out that he had been so anxious about them there across the river he'd almost started back alone.

Tien Pao's mother stopped tugging at her wet jacket to sit down heavily at that announcement. She began to cry. "Oh, Tien Pao! We didn't know what to do, where to go. We couldn't go across, even the footbridge is under. The river has risen so high with the rain—even the footbridge was under. And all we could hear was the river." She caught a deep breath. "Your father had gone to see if one of these river people would take him across —even they hesitated to cross in the dark, and they're river people. But you were going to cross alone!" Her voice sounded strangled. "Your father borrowed a lantern," she went on in a calmer voice. "He was in a state to seize one of these sampans and go after you, but then on top of the bank I heard the strange, foreign voice from the river. I called out, but you didn't answer. Oh, Tien Pao! And if the foreigner hadn't come back, you'd have tried to cross alone."

"It looks like my father is terribly angry," Tien Pao said solemnly to take her mind off the river dangers. He looked at the two hundred-yen notes squeezed in his hot, damp hand.

"Didn't he have reasons?" his mother burst out. "He worked all day swinging a heavy hammer, and nothing to eat all day. Then at the end of the long, hard day we found we would not even get one single yen—the Americans do not pay until the end of a week. Then the long, empty walk home in the rain. And then no sampan at the bank. And the river roaring in the dark . . ." She suddenly buttoned her jacket again. She reached out and took the yen notes from Tien Pao's hand. She looked at them. "Two hundred yen," she said softly. "It certainly turned out well. Why, I don't know. It must be the river god is still protecting the family of Tien. But if we are careful we can last out the week until the Americans pay." She became thoughtful. "Supper tonight—food! Charcoal for the stove, oil for the lamp, rice to grind for your baby sister," she recited.

She jumped up. "Your father's at one of the new neighbor's, arranging with him to keep our oars on his sampan—he will not trust you any more. I'm going to him at once. Tired as he is and hungry, he must get food and oil and charcoal. Why, then we can even dry our clothes! Maybe we can even afford a bit of tobacco for him. Oh, he'll go when he sees the two hundred yen. Everything will suddenly seem so much better. . . ." She laughed a little laugh, and hurried out of the sampan.

Tien Pao sighed and sat back with the baby sister. It had gone much better than he'd expected. Of course, there was still his father to face, but he felt immensely relieved. He hugged the baby. "Beauty-of-the-Republic," he said fondly over and over. "Beauty-of-the-Republic."

His mother came back into the sampan. "Your father's gone after food. You should have seen his big strides—especially when he heard me think aloud that maybe we could afford a bit of tobacco." She sounded almost gay. But then suddenly she was kneeling before Tien Pao, looking deep into his eyes. "Tien Pao, promise me you'll never take the sampan away from the bank again—not for anything or anybody!"

Tien Pao looked at her doubtfully. "But, Mother, if the airman should come again?"

She shook her head. "Not for two hundred yen —no, not for two hundred thousand yen could I go through it again. . . . Tien Pao, have you considered? What if you should try to cross and the river should take you?"

"The wonderful airman would help me row again," Tien Pao said sturdily.

"Tien Pao, do you know where the river would take you?" his mother said very slowly. "Suppose you risked it again! Suppose the terrible river current should wrench just one oar away. Your wonderful river-god airman has no experience with sampans. Tien Pao, do you know what would happen if the river took you and that American airman? Where it would take you? Back where we came from! Back to the Japanese! Do you know what would happen to your helpless airman? The Japanese would torture him—he is an airman. They would drive bamboo splinters under his tender nails until he told all about this great new field for airplanes we are building here at Hengyang. And when he had told, they would kill him."

Tien Pao went pale. He stared at his mother. His lips moved, but could make no sound. He shoved his fingers under him, sat on them. It was as if the torture pains were stabbing up under his fingernails, so real it seemed. "Mother," he whispered with difficulty, "never—never will I take the sampan away from the bank again."

His mother searched his face. "Then it is well," she said simply. "And if you'll tell your father that when he comes with the food, all will be well again."

CHAPTER TWO

SAMPAN IN THE RIVER

Early the next morning Tien Pao again watched his father and his mother, with the baby sister strapped to her back, clamber through the rain up the long, steep riverbank. Tien Pao stood in the opening of the sampan. "Remember now, you promised. Tomorrow I'm going with you to the great field for airplanes."

They did not hear him in the heavy rain. The sky was black with rain. It almost seemed as if the black sky were in the black river, and there was no sign of dawn. Tien Pao sighed, and shut himself up in the sampan behind the matting in the dreary, clammy dark. He looked wistfully toward the altar and the saucer lamp, but his mother had warned him not to waste oil in the long week before the Americans paid them for their work at the airfield.

The little pig was sleeping. The ducklings sat huddled in the bottom of their dry dishpan. Tien Pao lifted out the ducklings and went outside and scooped water out of the river into the dishpan. Maybe if the ducklings had water they'd start to swim and whisper their soft little peeps. It was so quiet. And if nothing moved, the long day would never move on.

Long before a little daylight came creeping over the river, Tien Pao had dragged out the rice mill, and had begun grinding some rice for the baby sister's evening meal. The dreary grinding at the stone mill seemed to make the time pass even slower, but it was something to do. Tien Pao went to fetch another handful of rice, later he fetched still another handful. He had to stop himself—if he ground any more, they'd all have to eat baby food for supper.

Now there was nothing left to do. Tien Pao was regretfully shoving the rice mill under the bench when a mighty thump sent the sampan crashing into the row of sampans. It knocked Tien Pao flat on his back. One of the ducklings spilled out of the dishpan with the splash of water that went over the side. The little pig jumped high and squealed in alarm.

Tien Pao scrambled to his feet. There were strange snortings right beside the sampan. Water gurgled and bubbled. Again there was a crash. Tien Pao clung to the bench with both hands. The other two ducklings splashed over the side in the new tidal wave in the dishpan. Tien Pao could not imagine what was happening. On hands and knees he crawled through the rocking boat, and pulled the mat out of the doorway. What he saw made him laugh. Five water buffaloes had come down the bank to wallow in the swollen river. Only their stretched, snorting noses and long flat horns were above the water. They were playing some kind of stupid cow game—pushing and ramming each other in the water.

Now again a rammed buffalo blundered backward into the sampan. The sampan rocked wildly on the water. They'd knock it loose from its moorings! Tien Pao reached back into the sampan, grabbed the dishpan, just letting the water splash. He waited for the first hard, bony rump to get within his reach. Then, yelling like mad, he crashed the empty pan down on a buffalo. The dishpan bonged like a temple gong. Five scared buffaloes reared up out of the water; they shoved each other out of the river and up the slippery bank with great alarmed snorts. They clambered clumsily, then the lead buffalo slipped and slid down the bank, bringing the others down. They piled up, heaved themselves to their feet again.

Dishpan in hand, Tien Pao stood laughing at the silly sight. He was still chuckling when he went back into the sampan, after having once more filled the dishpan with water from the river. He set the ducklings in the dishpan, replaced the mat in the doorway. He did not see that the stake by which the sampan was tied to the bank was lying on top of the rain-soaked ground. One of the buffaloes had blundered under the rope, had scraped it over his bony back, and had ripped the stake out of the soggy ground. The rope with the stake lay loose on the watery mud. Nothing held the sampan to the bank. Inside the sampan Tien Pao still sat chuckling. He had not seen it.

Tien Pao sat thinking out just how he'd tell the story of the buffaloes to his father and mother when they came home at night. It had been fun. He was almost sorry that he had scared the buffaloes away so soon. Now the long day loomed before him again.

Tien Pao sat awhile, then he imagined himself hungry. Sure, he felt a little hungry. It couldn't possibly be noon, but it was something to do. He

took down the bowl of cold rice his mother had prepared the day before and sat down with it on the floor. To make the simple meal last, he invented a game. He took the ducklings out of the dishpan and placed them around his rice bowl. The ducklings immediately began dipping their little flat bills into the rice. The faster Tien Pao dug with his chopsticks, the faster the ducklings pecked and gobbled. It became a race, but the rice was going too fast that way. The meal had to last.

Tien Pao had another idea. He tried to feed the ducklings with his chopsticks. He tried each duckling in turn, but it didn't work too well, and as he was absorbed with his chopsticks, the little pig unexpectedly rushed in and spoiled the whole game. The pig grabbed the lump of rice between the chopsticks, chopsticks and all. Tien Pao had to work to get the chopsticks from between his teeth. Then, with Tien Pao busy bending the chopsticks back into shape, the little pig pushed his snout into the rice bowl and snatched a big, greedy mouthful. In disgust Tien Pao elbowed the pig away, but there was nothing left in the bowl but a few crumbs. Tien Pao scattered the crumbs on the floor for the ducklings. For punishment he held the little pig over the crumbs, but just out of reach of the scattered rice. The little pig grunted in disgust and greed.

The miserable pig had ended the meal in one blow. Now there was absolutely nothing to do. The ducklings, back in their dishpan, already drifted in their huddled sleep. The pig lay stretched out on his side on the floor. Tien Pao decided he might as well sleep, too. What else was there to do? Using the pig for a pillow, he, too, stretched out on the floor.

He couldn't sleep. At least tomorrow he was going to the great field for airplanes. Tomorrow he'd at last see it, too. The thought made him restless, kept him awake. He tried to imagine from what he'd heard his father and mother say just what an airfield would be like. It seemed a bit odd—a big, grassy field for airplanes, as if they were horses or grazing goats. Tien Pao laughed too hard at the silly thought. It wasn't that funny. He began pestering the pig, tickling him on his undersides until the little pig could stand no more. With an annoyed squeal the pig jumped up. Tien Pao's head hit the floor.

In revenge for getting his head thumped, Tien Pao made a wild grab for the pig's hind leg. The little pig squealed wildly, managed to jerk away. He raced through the sampan. Now he seemed to want Tien Pao to chase him—he must be bored, too. But Tien Pao made believe he was sound asleep.

At last the impatient little pig edged back to Tien Pao, nudged him with his snout. Tien Pao reared up and let out such a crazy yell, the startled little animal almost fell over backward. A wild game began. They raced around the narrow sampan, Tien Pao yelling, the little pig squealing. The sampan rocked on the water with the commotion. It rocked, it inched forward, slid a little away from the bank. The galloping yelling game went on inside the sampan, and the sampan pulled from under its gangplank. The plank fell on the water with a hard, flat slap, but the yelling Tien Pao did not hear it.

At last the little pig could run no more. His sides heaved, he held his mouth wide open for breath. He threw himself down and lay where he fell. Tien Pao himself lay down, panting. He had to rest for a while.

Under the drumming of the rain on the matting there was not another sound anywhere. In all the sampans people seemed to have gone to sleep in the long, dull, rainy afternoon. Tien Pao fell asleep.

Quietly the shore end of the gangplank loosed itself from the slippery mud underneath the river-bank as the swollen river rose still higher with the rain. The plank scraped along the sampan; it edged out into the river, shot away as the river current caught it.

Almost as if the sampan had seen its gangplank race away and wanted to go after it, the sampan, too, loosed itself from the watery mud at the river's edge. First it drifted slowly, slowly it twirled. Slowly and quietly it edged along the row of sampans with the rope and stake dangling behind it. Then, like the plank, it was grabbed by the current. It shot away. It was swifter than the plank. It swept under a high, arched bridge. Under the bridge it passed the swiftly riding plank.

An old man under a silk umbrella stepped onto the bridge. In the rain darkness he saw a lone sampan sweeping away downriver. But the wind over the high bridge caught his umbrella. He pulled it down in front of his face and shuffled across the long bridge. When he looked again at the far end of the bridge, the sampan had disappeared. The old man looked at the racing river. He muttered to himself.

In the sampan Tien Pao woke up, but he was still too fuzzy with sleep to get up. From where he lay he idly tried to peer through a crack in the matting at the riverbank to see if it was nearly dark, and if it was almost time for his father and mother to come. It felt as if he'd slept long.

He rubbed his eyes. But it was dark! Darker than rain dark. A rushing sound was in his ears! There wasn't any matting at the back of the sampan. The wind had ripped the matting away. There wasn't any riverbank! This was the night! This was the river! This was the sampan rushing headlong down the roaring river in the night!

Tien Pao jumped up. He clutched the side of the racing sampan.

"Mother!"

The wind caught up his shriek, but lost it in the rain.

"MOTHER!"

Tien Pao began to cry. Then he hopelessly still yelled out one word:

"FATHER!"

He suddenly was still. Hopeless, numb with fear, he sank to the bottom of the sampan. He did not dare shout again. It was no use. His mother and father couldn't possibly hear. But the Japanese could hear! The river was taking him back—back to the Japanese. With a terrified whimper Tien Pao caught the little pig to him. He shook the pig awake—shook him hard. Then he held him so hard, the little pig groaned.

Outside there were only the night and the roaring river and the rain. Wide-eyed and unseeing, Tien Pao stared into the darkness, clutching his pig. He hugged the little pig until his arms ached. The ache in his throat stayed, but he could not cry. He whispered something to the pig. The words made no sense, they had no meaning, but it made him feel a little better to whisper to someone. He did it again. He said: "Beauty-of-the-Republic." He whispered it once more as a hard, hurting sob came breaking out of his throat. Tien Pao heard his own whispered words, he wondered at himself for a brief, fleeting moment. He'd said: "Beauty-of-the-Republic." He'd called the pig by the name of his baby sister. It was silly, babyish, naming a pig that.

No, it wasn't! It felt safer being with something that had a name. He said it aloud: "Beauty-of-the-Republic." And somehow it felt safer.

But the little pig, tired of his odd position, wriggled out of Tien Pao's arms, jumped to the floor, scampered to the back of the sampan. "Beauty-of-the-Republic!" Tien Pao screamed as he lunged after him. He grabbed him by a hind leg, dragged him back. The little pig let out a long, loud squeal. It scared Tien Pao. He caught the pig's snout, held it so fiercely, the little pig had to struggle and scratch and fight to get breath.

"I mustn't yell, and you mustn't scream," Tien Pao whispered in his ear. "And you can't jump to the bank—there isn't any bank." With the pig under his arm he crawled to the back of the sampan and pulled in the rope. He crawled back. He kept the little pig pinched between his legs while he unknotted the rope and removed the stake. He doubled the rope, tied one end to the pig's front leg and the other end around his own wrist.

"We have to stay together," he earnestly whispered. "We might hit something and smash. We've got to stay together." He reached back into the sampan, found the dishpan in the dark, and pulled it tightly against him. He and the pig and ducklings sat in a tight huddle in the center of the sampan.

The little pig began grunting sleepily. Tien Pao could not let him sleep. He shook him fiercely, but then in regret held him snug in his arms again. "Beauty-of-the-Republic," he pleaded. He looked fondly down at the little pig. Somehow calling him that and holding him made it feel a little bit as if he still had a family. And now it didn't sound crazy or silly. But he shouldn't call a pig by his own little sister's name. "I'll call you—Glory-of-the-Republic," Tien Pao decided. He peered at the ducklings peeping sleepily in their dishpan. Glory-of-the-Republic and the ducklings—they were his family. It was better, much better than being alone, storming down the river in the pitch-black sampan. "Glory-of-the-Republic, we've got to stay together,"

Tien Pao said tenderly. In the dark he tested the knots in the rope.

The wind began to blow. The wind rushed in with the rain, swept it through the sampan from one end to the other. Tien Pao turned his back to the lashing rain, bowed his head. Dimly he could see the little mirror in the altar to the river god. His lips moved. "River god—good river god, the wind. The wind! Make it push the sampan to shore."

Later the wind on the river must have changed, as the sampan seemed to rush in a great, sweeping curve. Tien Pao was almost sure that now the sampan was racing into another river. But in the new river the wind fell down from the mountains, crashed down on the sampan in one shrieking blow. In one blow it tore the arched roof of mats off the sampan, flung them up, flung them down into the river. The mirror of the altar to the river god smashed to bits on the floor. The sampan rushed along wide open to the sky and slashing rain and wind. Rain hurled against the wooden floor.

Down from the mountains the rain came in sheets, in torrents. In one moment Tien Pao was soaked. He crawled under the bench—there was no other place to crawl for shelter. He crouched under the bench on hands and knees and pulled Glory-of-the-Republic under him to shelter him from the hard, beating rain. He pulled the dishpan before him, kept his hands clenched around the rim.

The rain water rose fast in the open sampan. Under him Glory-of-the-Republic uttered distressed little grunts, but the numbed Tien Pao kept the rope short, kept him where he was. He felt the water flowing over his hands clenched around the dishpan, crawling up his wrists. Now the three ducklings flowed out of the dishpan with the rising rain water. They swam about happily in their new big pool. One behind the other they swam in excited, whispering circles through the sampan. Suddenly their peeping stopped, they became very busy. They dived and dipped. Tien Pao could hear the tiny clatter of their bills along the floor under the water.

At first he paid no attention. Suddenly he pushed the pig out of his way. The ducklings were diving for rice! The water had reached the little shelf under the bench and was washing all the ground rice away. All the rice was lost! His only food! But if the water had reached the shelf, it could sink the sampan. Tien Pao grabbed the dishpan and wildly started bailing the rain water overboard. He had a scare when he almost scooped a diving duckling overboard with the water. He went at it more quietly, forced himself to make no loud scraping sounds.

When at last the dishpan began touching the bottom, Tien Pao tried to save some of the gritty rice that had settled to the floor. He found his rice bowl. He drained the watery rice through his fingers, feeling carefully for any glass splinters from the shattered mirror. Crumb by pasty crumb he gathered a half-bowlful of wet rice.

And while Tien Pao worked like that, the rain stopped and light came—morning came to the river.

In the first glimmer of the dawn Tien Pao saw the dim, far banks. It was a wide river. It was three times wider than the river at Hengyang. But when Tien Pao peered ahead under the morning mists floating up from the river, the great river swept into a still wider river. Rivers, Tien Pao knew, widen as they near the sea. And near the sea were the Japanese. Tien Pao's scalp crawled with horror.

Where the two rivers finally met, Tien Pao saw a village loom up in the misty dawn. His own village had been at the corner of two rivers! His mouth dry with fear, Tien Pao stared at the distant village. It couldn't be his village! The Japanese had burned his village to the ground, but in this village the houses still stood.

The sampan swung into the new river. The village came closer. But this wasn't a living village! The houses weren't houses. They were empty, blackened, roofless walls. His village! And there, pacing slowly back and forth along the riverbank, was a Japanese soldier. Behind the sentry lay the gutted village.

Tien Pao crouched low in the sampan, but he couldn't keep himself from peering fearfully over the edge. The soldier stopped, stood looking up the river. He took his rifle down. To Tien Pao, crouched in the approaching sampan, it seemed that the soldier was looking right at him—that a shot must come. He couldn't take his horrified eyes off the soldier. But the sentry merely shifted his rifle to the other shoulder and began pacing again.

It broke the horror spell, and as the sentry shifted the gun, Tien Pao made his move. He slid himself flat in the watery bottom of the sampan. He mustn't crouch, mustn't stare over the edge. He kept one arm tightly over the pig so he wouldn't move. Nothing must move. It must be that the rain mists sifting over the river toward the shore had hidden the flat, roofless sampan from the staring sentry, but the rain was over, the mist was lifting, clear bright light was coming to the river. Nothing must move.

As he lay there motionless, his back exposed to the open sky went rigid with dread. It was again as if he heard the airplanes screaming over the treetops, the stutter of bullets, the whining, biting hail of bullets in the water. He fought an almost insane urge to keep his eyes on the sentry. He hid his face in the crook of his arm, and lay still again.

It seemed hours before Tien Pao at last allowed himself to lift his head and fearfully look back. The village was gone. This was new country completely unknown to him. Tien Pao looked ahead. The river had become fearfully wide—wide and straight. It must be going straight to the sea now. With the wideness of the river the current had spread, the sampan seemed to move more slowly. Straight ahead was a deep bay in the bank of the river—there the water seemed almost quiet. Tien Pao grabbed the dishpan. Stretching flat on his face in the back of the sampan, he held the dishpan at a sharp angle down in the water. With the dishpan as a rudder, the sampan slowly began to respond. Slowly, in a seemingly endless curve, it turned toward the quiet bay. At last the sampan rode into the wide, shallow bay. There was a scraping of sand and gravel as it ground to a stop near the shore.

Tien Pao scooped up the swimming ducklings and set them in the dishpan in the river. He grabbed the little pig, the bowl of watery rice, and jumped into the shallow water. With the rice bowl in one hand, pushing the dishpan ahead of him with the other hand, and tugging Glory-of-the-Republic, splashing snout-deep, behind him, Tien Pao hurried to the silent shore.

The ducklings in the dishpan peered up at Tien Pao with their black beads of eyes; they peeped excited little whispers up at him. Tien Pao stopped. But he couldn't carry a dishpan and ducklings over the mountains! Ducklings were food. If he wrung their necks, he could sling them over his shoulder, and he'd have food for days.

The thought of the three ducklings hanging limp over his shoulder was all of a sudden too much for Tien Pao. He looked at the ducklings, then he shut his eyes tight and gave the dishpan a hard shove back into the bay. Without looking back, Tien Pao climbed up from the river and up the first rocky cliff.

On top of the cliff Tien Pao turned. The empty sampan had pulled back into the current; it was going down the river. Below in the bay the white dishpan drifted and twirled. Two ducklings swam in the dishpan, but one must have gone overboard with Tien Pao's hard, blind shove. The little duckling was chasing the dishpan, scrambling desperately to get out of the big river back into its little dishpan home. When he saw that, Tien Pao's lips trembled. He turned away, and looked no more toward the river.

CHAPTER THREE

NIGHT IN THE MOUNTAINS

They weren't hills, they weren't mountains; but, hills or mountains, all that mattered to Tien Pao and the little pig that trudged beside him was that they were terribly hard to climb. The going down among the rocks and brush was almost as hard as the going up. The early dawn when Tien Pao had shoved the dishpan with the ducklings back into the river seemed far away and long ago. The rain was falling steadily again, but though Tien Pao had traveled long, his own village had not loomed up again out of the rain gloom. For that one thing the exhausted Tien Pao felt dumbly grateful. He hoped he had gone far around it.

It must be afternoon. Tien Pao still clutched the bowl of watery rice, but he did not dare stop to eat.

He was hungry, he was exhausted, but he did not dare to stop to rest. There were paths in the little mountains, but Tien Pao did not dare to use them. Coolies came down those paths, and farmers. Once from his height among the rocks Tien Pao had even seen a Japanese soldier hurrying down a distant path. And once he had seen a woman like his mother. Even her walk had been like his mother's walk—tall, straight, and willow-slim. His heart pounding, Tien Pao had watched her, and everything in him had wanted him to run down to her, to tell her what had happened to him, and to ask her what to do. But he'd kept his distance, he'd kept himself hidden while he watched her out of sight.

He still did not trust himself to go among his own people. He did not know whether it would be safe in this country that the Japanese had taken over. Perhaps the Japanese soldier would have paid no more attention to him than he had to the other Chinese that he had passed on the path, but Tien Pao didn't know.

In the late afternoon Tien Pao suddenly could go no farther. He broke into a cold sweat, his legs trembled under him, he was nauseated with hunger. He had reached the top of a round, grassy hill. There were a few sheltering bushes, and he crawled behind them. He had to eat, had to rest. He dug his hand into the rice bowl and gulped a choking big mouthful. Glory-of-the-Republic began tearing at the grass. Tien Pao dug his hand into the bowl again, stuffed his mouth full. Again his hand went to the bowl. He pulled it back. There was only a good handful of rice left in the bottom of the bowl. He mustn't touch it, mustn't eat it—he mustn't keep looking at it! It had to be saved for one more meal.

He heard voices. He peered through the bushes. A group of boys and girls were coming up the hill with baskets on their backs and grass knives in their hands. They came slowly and weakly—like old people. They even looked like old people! The skin was drawn like old paper over their cheekbones. The children stopped halfway up the hill, put their baskets down, and began sawing at the sparse grass with their hooked knives. Those children ate grass! They stuffed whole handfuls into their

mouths before they put as much as a blade of grass into their baskets. Then one little boy began to eat mud!

Tien Pao looked on, horrified. The mud-eating boy was the smallest of the lot. He kept away from the others, as if he were ashamed. He dragged himself around behind his bloated, huge stomach. His sticks of legs looked silly under that big stomach. And now the little boy scooped up a handful of dirt again and brought it to his mouth. His sister saw it, and scolded him in a tired, old way. The other children looked up, but did not seem to care. The little fellow hung his head. He slowly opened his hand and let the mud dribble out of it. He looked at his empty, dirty hand and began to cry.

Tien Pao looked on—sickened. His glance went from the skeleton boy with the bloated stomach to the sturdy little pig beside him. Suddenly he was desperately afraid. Glory-of-the-Republic was food! He was in danger from these starving people. If those children down the hill saw the little pig, they would fall on him and tear him to pieces. They'd drink his warm blood.

The little shamed boy who had eaten the dirt had thrown himself down and lay, face hidden in his arm, sobbing. The other children had gone out of sight around the side of the hill. Tien Pao could stand it no longer. He took Glory-of-the-Republic by the rope and stole toward the crying boy. Without a sound he set the rice bowl on the ground close to the little fellow's head. When he'd at last look up from his hungry, shamed crying—he'd see food!

Tien Pao started to steal away, but ten paces beyond the little boy he broke into a hard run. He had to run even though these starved, weak children couldn't possibly catch him and Glory-of-the-Republic. He and the pig raced down the hill and up and over the next one. Tien Pao wasn't weary any more, he wasn't hungry. He wanted to rush on and on, over this rocky hill and the next, far from this country and the evil the Japanese had brought to it.

Glory-of-the-Republic could not stand the pace, or he did not like it. He began dragging on the end of the rope, and he tried to grab mouthfuls of grass in passing. Tien Pao would not let him. He did not dare stop for anything now. For now he remembered other things. All this rainy day he had not seen one little black goat. Always before the little black goats had capered in the mountains. He had not seen a single ox in a field, a pig in a yard, nor a water buffalo in a single rice paddy below the mountains. There hadn't even been one lean dog on any mountain path, or around the mud huts among the paddies. It could only mean that the

Japanese had taken everything from the people, and the hungry people had eaten the dogs.

But if the Japanese had taken everything, he wasn't safe in these hills with a pig! The thought stopped Tien Pao in his tracks. He wasn't safe in daylight! He'd merely been lucky so far this dark rainy day, but the Japanese had but to get one glimpse of him with a pig, and they'd know he wasn't from this wasted land. Here were no pigs! Tien Pao stared desperately around him from the tall rock on which he was standing. He did not know what to do. He wanted to rush away from this horrible country, but it would be dangerous to take another step in daylight—sooner or later he and his pig would be seen.

Glory-of-the-Republic rooted about while Tien Pao stood hesitating. The little pig snorted and dug. Leaves rustled at Tien Pao's feet, pebbles rattled. He became so noisy, it finally aroused Tien Pao's attention. He looked down. Right at his feet Glory-of-the-Republic had shoved himself under a rock ledge. He'd almost disappeared, only his curly excited tail still showed. Under the ledge was a little cave. The little pig had found a cave! Suddenly Tien Pao knew what to do—hide in little caves by day, and travel by night!

He dropped to hands and knees beside the rooting pig, helped him dig out the collected leaves and debris until the cave was big enough. After a long look all around to see that no one had observed them, Tien Pao squirmed into the opening with Glory-of-the-Republic. It was a narrow little hole, but Tien Pao reached out and scraped all the leaves back into the entrance. When the cave's opening was completely closed with leaves, Tien Pao and his pig stretched out behind them to wait for the coming of night.

It was a horrible, tense feeling, lying in a hole in a rock in the daytime, waiting and listening. But the little cave was high, and far from any path. Gradually, as not a single sound penetrated the wall of leaves, Tien Pao began to feel safer. No one was near. No one had passed the mouth of the cave. Tien Pao eased his tense, rain-soaked body.

Gradually a little warm light began filtering through the leaves. The cave was becoming snug, warm almost. But warmth—light! That meant the sun! The sun must have come out. After all the days the rain at last had stopped. Outside, the sun was shining.

The comfort of the sun warmth, the stillness, the waiting brought a new sick gnawing. All in a moment Tien Pao went sick with longing for his mother and his father and the baby sister. The desperation grew so strong Tien Pao had to fight himself to keep from bursting through the leaves and start running home—impossible as it was. The homesickness gnawed at his insides like a huge, relentless rat. He mustn't cry—crying made noise. He mustn't—he wasn't a baby! Suddenly Tien Pao shoved his face hard against the little pig's side to stifle his sobs. In the muffled cave behind the leaves, his face pressed against the sleeping pig, Tien Pao had to let go, had to cry himself out. And then he slept. And while he slept, night fell.

It was deep, dark night when Tien Pao awoke. He cautiously pushed away some of the leaves and peered out of the cave. The mountains lay in black silence. Tien Pao listened long. Then to his ears came a slight sound, and the blood started pounding in his ears. He clung to his pig. Something was coming in the dark, came running—running straight toward him and the cave. Tien Pao's heart stood still. Long, frozen moments later he began to realize that the soft running sound was the sound of the river. Why, of course, below the mountains ran the river! And then Tien Pao could manage a hollow little laugh at himself. He laughed at himself again, a little louder. It somehow made him feel bolder.

Now that he knew what it was, the running sound of the river actually made him feel safer. It was the river. Somehow in running wildly away from the children on the grassy hill, he had blundered back to the river. The sound of the river was good. It was a guide. He must never go away from the sound of the river, Tien Pao decided. Since he'd have to travel by night, the river's sound would have to lead him home. Oh, the sound of the river was good! The river had taken him away, the river would take him back—back to Hengyang and his mother and his father and the baby sister. Tien Pao mumbled a little prayer to the river god. The good river god! "Bring me home. Bring me safely home."

As if he could still reach home that night, Tien Pao grabbed the rope, pushed himself out of the cave, and pulled the unwilling, sleep-warm pig out after him. Together they started out through the little black mountains.

Five nights later Tien Pao and Glory-of-the-Republic were still in the little river mountains. The going was painfully slow. Tien Pao forced himself up still another steep mountain path. His knees buckled under him. He had the little pig slung over his shoulder, but it was too much, he was too weak with hunger. But he had to carry Glory-of-the-Republic. The little pig was not made to climb mountains. The sharp rocks cut his feet, grinding gravel dug between his narrow, cloven hoofs. His feet were bleeding.

Tien Pao felt his way up the path. He pulled himself up by the jutting rock wall that loomed over him. His fingers touched a bunch of grass, he tore it up by the roots and brought it to his mouth. The gritty grass under his teeth nauseated him. He gave it to the little pig on his shoulder. At least Glory-of-the-Republic could eat grass. He could eat, but he couldn't walk. Soon, Tien Pao knew, he himself would not be able to walk any more. The hunger gnawed too fiercely. It burned and gnawed all night long, every slow step of the back-breaking way. It never let up, it only dulled when, stupefied with exhaustion, he slept in some little cave.

Halfway up the steep path Tien Pao had to set the pig down. Enormous ballooning black spots came swimming before his eyes. He backed away until he felt a rock, he leaned against it. Cold, clammy sweat stood out on him. He pulled his eyes wide with his fingers to make the awful lilting spots go away. Still they ballooned before his eyes, darker than the night—an evil dark. They were everywhere. They were above him and before him, huge, threatening, closing in on him.

It must be hunger. It was only hunger. It was only that he was weak and dizzy from hunger. That's what made the spots. There wasn't really anything else. Tien Pao shook his head to clear it, but fear clamped his heart. He wasn't alone. They

were still there—things on the path! Spirits? Were these the evil spirits of the mountains he'd often heard about in his village? The old people kept talking about them and their horror. How they hid in caves, oozed out of rocks. Now they were coming for him!

They had waited until he was weak, but now they were everywhere. Leering down at him from all the rocks! Lilting, lifting, reaching out. Tien Pao tried to shake away the terror. They weren't real! It was only because he was so weak and hungry. They kept coming. Tien Pao tore his eyes away from the coming horror, looked down. The little pig wasn't beside him! Glory-of-the-Republic was gone. Without a sound they'd gotten Glory-of-the-Republic!

With a cry of terror Tien Pao broke and ran. He ran with the mad strength of terror, blindly, headlong down the mountain. The evil came right on behind him—rattling rocks, sharp crunching gravel rolled at his heels. Tien Pao threw himself ahead of the rattling sounds. He could hear panting. It kept coming—at his heels.

Tien Pao could not keep up his headlong speed down the mountain. He tripped, he hurtled into space, with a great, scary splash he was flung headlong into water. Gasping with the shock, Tien Pao struggled to a sitting position in the muddy water. But water—mud! Then this was a rice paddy. But then he was out of the mountains. Then he was safe from the terrible spirits of the mountains. A rice paddy! Tien Pao almost lay back in it as if it were a bed, so great was his relief. He breathed deep.

All of a sudden something nudged Tien Pao's arm. Tien Pao reared up out of the water. It was Glory-of-the-Republic! They hadn't got Glory-of-the-Republic! Why, it must have been the little pig that had come bowling on behind him in his wild flight down the mountain. That was why the gravel had rattled—that was the panting. Foolish with relief, Tien Pao sat back in the water and pulled the little pig into his lap. Why, all the time it had been his own wonderful pig—not spirits!

Glory-of-the-Republic was far more interested in the muddy paddy than in being gratefully petted. He squirmed free, and grunting happily he wallowed up to his nostrils in the oozy mud. Tien Pao fondly watched him, and watching the pig gave Tien Pao a good, useful idea.

It was easy to sit here in the rice paddy below the mountain and not be too afraid of the mountain spirits. But he had to go back up into the mountains. This was a rice paddy, and rice paddies meant that people were near. Tien Pao could dimly see the shadowy wall of a village compound looming up beyond the misty paddies. Japanese soldiers might be quartered right behind that wall. He had to go up. Maybe there weren't spirits in the mountains. Maybe it was only his hunger that made him see things that weren't there, but Tien Pao couldn't convince himself. He quailed at the thought of going up into the mountains.

There was only one thing to do—do what Glory-of-the-Republic had done, wallow in the mud, disguise himself with mud and try to fool the mountain spirits so they wouldn't recognize him as the same weak, exhausted boy when he climbed back among them. Tien Pao brought up mud from the bottom of the paddy and plastered his face with the oozy, syrupy, reeking stuff. He rolled himself in it. With bluish, vile mud dripping from him Tien Pao stood up and studied the little pig critically. He was encouraged. The thick mud must fool the spirits! Why, Glory-of-the-Republic looked like nothing but a mud ball with four mud legs. If his own plaster of mud was as good, the mountain spirits wouldn't think he was human; they'd never recognize him as the same scared, weak, hungry boy. The mud was thick enough, but it was still a thin hope. Still, he had to go up.

Quaking with fear, Tien Pao began the long ascent. But as he climbed, he realized he was weaker than ever after his mad, headlong dash, and he was terrified. There they were again, darker than the rock darkness—swelling, lilting, lifting. Waiting for him on the upward path, reaching down for him.

It was hunger. There wasn't anything in the darkness.

"It's hunger," Tien Pao yelled up into the mountains. The rocks echoed it back. From far above him his distorted voice came mocking back as if something were laughing at him. "It's only hunger,"

Tien Pao whispered to the little pig. "That's all. There's nothing. There really is nothing."

He kept whispering it to the little pig, as if the little pig had to be convinced, as if the pig were scared. It did not help, he could not force himself to take another upward step. He stood sick with fear, listening, watching. And then he suddenly realized it—he was also lost. He was lost! In his wild dash down the mountainside he had lost the guiding sound of the river. The river was gone. Instead there was a new sound. There it was again—a rumbling in the valley far beyond the rice paddies and the cluster of dim houses. Tien Pao tried to puzzle out the distant sound, but in the evil, brooding silence right around him his mind was too numb with fear to think. He eyed the looming mountain again. Oh, if only he did not have to go up!

The next moment Tien Pao forgot the rumbling in the valley. A sleeping cuckoo called in a muffled, dreamy voice among the rocks right above him. Glory-of-the-Republic was rustling in loose gravel, snuffling out a cave where he could find leaves to eat. The friendly, homely sounds reassured Tien Pao.

Again the muffled cuckoo called, but now it was higher in the mountains. Tien Pao pulled Glory-of-the-Republic out of the little cave. With the friendly cuckoo calling above him as if leading him on, Tien Pao thought he dared to go up. It took all his strength to lift Glory-of-the-Republic to his shoulder, but they had to go up now or he'd never dare. Tien Pao took one step up the steep path, and then he pitched forward. Glory-of-the-Republic hurtled off his shoulder to the rocky path. The little pig uttered a short, piercing scream, and was still.

The sharp squeal of the pig roused Tien Pao from his momentary faint. There lay Glory-of-the-Republic across the path, his four legs stretched out stiff and straight. Dead! Oh, not dead! Tien Pao crawled on hands and knees to his little pig. He blindly felt for the cave where Glory-of-the-Republic had been rooting. He pulled himself and the silent pig inside. "Oh, not dead, not dead!"

Tien Pao kept praying but he could not force himself to make sure whether the little pig was dead or just stunned. He could not let himself think about the nights ahead without the little pig. To go on alone in the dark through the evil blackness in the silent, brooding mountains—he couldn't do it! Tien Pao kept frantically stuffing the mouth of the cave with leaves to keep himself from thinking. He hardly noticed that the leaves were wet and soggy. Dumbly, hopelessly, he kept building a wall of leaves.

Behind him in the cave there was a muffled

sound. Tien Pao whirled. There stood Glory-of-the-Republic—on his four feet! He wasn't dead—he was eating leaves! Tien Pao grabbed him and babbled words into the little pig's twitching ear. He almost crushed him. Glory-of-the-Republic grunted and wriggled free and hurried back to his meal of leaves.

Tien Pao could hardly do it, but he had to stop the little pig. These leaves were so wet, they packed down so tightly, he had to keep every leaf for the little wall he had built up in the mouth of the cave. Tien Pao pulled four handfuls from the inside of the wall of leaves. "There—but that's all you can have."

He sat listening almost wistfully to the little pig gobbling leaves. Suddenly he pulled a handful out of the little wall. He sniffed at the wet handful. Maybe leaves tasted better than grass. He closed his eyes and shoved some into his mouth. He smacked his lips loudly to make himself believe the soggy, musty mess tasted good. He swallowed them. They were bitter as gall, but at once they helped. For a moment his fierce hunger left him. He opened his eyes. His eyes had cleared! The spots were gone—the ballooning, lilting spots had gone away. Tien Pao grabbed another handful of leaves.

Almost at the same moment that his hunger

gnawings were stilled, Tien Pao became unbearably weary and sleepy. He couldn't force his eyes to stay open. He still tried to plaster some wet leaves on Glory-of-the-Republic's head where he thought it must be sore from the fall, but the little pig promptly shook them off and ate them. Tien Pao stared hard at the little pig, and in a sleepy, heavy way he pondered that the leaves might do Glory-of-the-Republic even more good from the inside than from the outside. Before he had finished the ponderous thought, he was sound asleep. He did not hear the cuckoo call.

CHAPTER FOUR

THE RIVER CLIFF

Steadily through the night, water trickled into the cave. It backed up behind the wall of leaves Tien Pao had plastered in the opening. The water seeping over the cold rock on which they were lying distressed Glory-of-the-Republic. He snuffled unhappily, and nudged Tien Pao. Tien Pao did not stir from his exhausted sleep. The little pig climbed onto his chest to get out of the wet. He rolled off the moment he fell asleep. He rolled through the wall of leaves into the open. He immediately began eating the leaves.

Light filtering through the opening at last roused

Tien Pao. He sat up in alarm. He was soaked through and through, chilled to the bone. His teeth chattering, he cautiously poked his head out of the little cave. Dawn was glimmering in the sky. It shimmered in the river. But that was the river! He had not lost the river after all! It had been there all the time, but its soft rustling had been drowned out last night by the heavy rumble he had heard in the valley.

When he could keep his teeth from chattering, Tien Pao heard it again—the same steady, unending rumble of the night before. He crept stiffly from the cave, and looked into the lightening sky. It looked as if it were going to be a bright, clear day. Whatever it was down there below, there was no time to lose if they were to find another cave to hide in before full sunlight burst over the mountains. They couldn't stay in this watery hole—they'd freeze or drown.

Tien Pao had difficulty holding his shivering body still while he looked about him to size up the situation. The little cave into which he had blundered last night was in the side of a towering cliff that rose like a poking finger tall and solitary into the sky. A narrow path corkscrewed past the cave and up the steep back of the cliff. The path must lead on through the mountains, and somewhere along it must certainly be some little cave for hiding.

A dry little cave, Tien Pao hoped fervently—on the sunny side of the cliff, he added to his hope. He shivered, and flexed his stiff, aching body. The rumble down below came stronger to his ears. It worried him. He hastily undid the rope to give the little pig full freedom to find a cave, then they hurried up the cliff. Day was dawning.

They climbed higher and higher up the tall cliff, and as they climbed, they searched. Glory-of-the-Republic dug and snuffled. Tien Pao poked into every likely-looking crevice. There seemed to be no other cave in this sharp, solitary cliff. They hurried on up. They rounded a turn in the twisting path. It proved to be the last turn. Tien Pao and Glory-of-the-Republic were on top of the peak. The domed top was smooth and bald, like the old head of an old man. There was nothing on the rounded dome but a lone thorn bush and a huge boulder, worn smooth and polished. Tien Pao looked at it in dismay. The high peak was nothing but a lookout point. The path had led to nothing but the big boulder polished and worn by generations that had come here to sit and look down at the valley and the river. The rumble in the valley beat up against the lone cliff. Morning sunlight reflected off the polished boulder.

Full daylight—there was no time to lose. In full sunshine they'd have to rush all the way down the cliff, climb up a farther mountain, and then still find a cave to hide in. Unless there might be a cave somewhere on the river side of this peak. Tien Pao hurried over the dome to the thorn bush for a quick look.

What he saw below him made him gasp. The high cliff jutted out over the river; straight underneath him glistened the water. But across the river in the deep river valley was a road. From that road came the endless rumble. Huge trucks were grinding down that road, bumper to bumper. Dust clouds rolled up behind the trucks. Now into the dust of the trucks came a troop of galloping horses. Soldiers with rifles sat straight and proud on the backs of the horses. Behind these mounted troops came horses pulling cannon—six horses to a cannon. The Japanese were on the move! They were going the same way he was going—toward Hengyang?

As the stunned Tien Pao stood looking down on this scene from behind the thorn bush, the men on the cannon all of a sudden began whipping their horses. The troop of horsemen leaned over the necks of their horses and thundered on into the dust behind the trucks. The trucks rolled faster. The grinding of the trucks whined up against the cliff.

The Japanese soldiers were looking up. They twisted their necks and looked up into the sky, and the air over the river was so clear and bright, it looked almost as if they were staring right at Tien Pao on top of the cliff. Tien Pao, too, twisted his neck and looked up into the sky behind him. There in the morning sky a speck appeared. It was like the speck a hawk makes when he sails over the yard of a farmer where chickens are pecking the straw. But it wasn't a high speck any more. It was a swift, high airplane. And now it fell screaming out of the sky toward the trucks and the horses.

Down below, the trucks were not riding packed together any more—they were strung out along the road. Horsemen had tumbled off their horses and lay along the road, their rifles pointing to the sky. But the men on the cannon still came on, they leaned far out, they lashed their horses on.

All in one screaming moment the airplane was above the road and along the road. Low now—big and snarling. Then it happened as it had happened at Tien Pao's village. This airplane, too, came with a horrible stuttering screech of bullets, but this was not against a peaceful Chinese village and helpless sampans—this was against the Japanese.

Some of the trucks stopped, some of the drivers threw themselves into the rice paddies along the road. Some of the trucks rolled on into the hail of bullets and explosions. A truck turned over, its wheels thrashing the air like the many feet of a great, clumsy bug. A truck burst into flames and stopped; the truck behind crashed into it with a sound of thunder. The driver pitched through the glass into the flames of the truck ahead.

In flashing swiftness the airplane and its hail of bullets were beyond the trucks. The plane came back. It zigzagged from one side of the road to the other to catch the horses and men running into the fields. The awful, unearthly scream of horses rent the air and beat against the cliff. Tien Pao dug his fingers into his ears, but it was as if the screaming went on inside him. His skin went tight with horror, but he kept looking, he couldn't tear his eyes away.

Men fell, horses fell. Men tumbled off cannon and the cannon went over them behind the madly plunging horses. Horses broke loose from their traces and reared and floundered in the deep, muddy ooze of the rice paddies. One, wounded and maddened, thrashed over the bank into the river and sank from sight. The river turned red where the horse had gone under.

But not all of the men who lay along the road lay still. Some raised rifles and fired at the low-sweeping plane. Bullets smacked into it, and once the plane jerked queerly as if it had stumbled in the air. But it rose, the way a great wounded bird swoops up, shaking itself. Higher it climbed, higher, in a straight zooming upward line toward a peaceful cloudbank drifting over the river.

Before the plane could quite reach the cloudbank a black mass of smoke belched out of it. For a moment it was hidden from Tien Pao's sight in its own black smoke. But only for a moment. The next moment the plane came falling through the smoke, down toward the road and the river.

Tien Pao squeezed his eyes shut. He trembled. He could not bear to see the helpless plane spinning and whistling down to the earth. His fists clenched and unclenched.

Then a new sound came to Tien Pao's ears, the sound of a motor coughing. When he opened his eyes the airplane had somehow straightened out of its helpless dive. It was going down, but it spun no longer. Somehow it found the road. Somehow it leaped and bumped down onto the road, bounced along it with the swiftness of light. It stopped too soon! It stopped too short! Its tail flew up and flipped over. There lay the plane on its helpless back. A roaring mass of yellow flames gushed out of it.

On top of the cliff Tien Pao could not breathe. There lay the flaming plane. No one could be alive in that! But out of the flames a man came tumbling. His clothes were on fire. He tumbled and rolled away from the plane, and he beat at his clothes with his bare hands. He jumped up, ripped off the

aviator's helmet that was smoldering at the back of his neck, and beat at the flames with that. But was that the airman? Was it the yellow-haired airman he had rowed across the river—his river god? Tien Pao could not believe it. With his eyes riveted on the man, he talked to Glory-of-the-Republic about it—short little unbelieving words. It couldn't be. Oh, it couldn't be. He had seen only the one airman—maybe all Americans had yellow hair. It must be that.

In the valley the Japanese had started running. They jumped up from everywhere and ran toward the distant burning plane. The airman crouched in the bushes, still beating at his smoldering clothes.

"Run! Run!" Tien Pao wanted to shout. "RUN!"

He must not shout—he dared not shout.

As if the yellow-haired airman had heard the

shout Tien Pao had not shouted, he suddenly backed away into the bushes. The first two Japanese came racing down the road toward him. They did not know anything alive had come out of those flames. In the bushes a pistol gleamed. It spat. And again! The two Japanese fell on the open road. But others were coming, and the white soldier knew it, for now he broke from the bushes and ran toward the river. But he was so slow! He must run faster. Faster! Then Tien Pao saw that he dragged his leg. Now he stopped, he clung to a bamboo clump for support. Now he limped off again in his crouching run.

He did not run straight. He kept clumps of bushes and bamboo between him and the Japanese. Now he started on the last short sprint to the river-bank. Two Japanese came around a bamboo clump. The white soldier threw himself flat. Then his pistol barked. One Japanese fell, but the other crawled on, hidden by the bamboo. And as he crawled he held his pistol ready, but he did not shoot. By that Tien Pao knew that the Japanese were trying to take the airman alive. And he remembered what his mother had told him: if they caught him they would torture him—bamboo splinters under the fingernails. The crawling torture pains stabbed up into Tien Pao's fingers again the way they had done when he had sat before his mother on the bench in the sampan. And there was nothing he could do for the airman—nothing.

But the airman had known about the second Japanese. There was a shot. The Japanese let slip his hold on the bamboo clump, and sagged. The airman turned to dive into the river. It was a trick. It was a trick! Didn't the airman know—didn't he see? The Japanese was coming around the bamboo—in one bounding leap clearing the space between him and the airman on the bank.

Before he realized he was doing it, Tien Pao was screaming out: "LOOK OUT! LOOK OUT!"

It was Chinese, but it was a warning scream, and that the airman understood. He whirled, he shot. It was all one motion, but this time the Japanese crumpled, and this time it was no trick. And now the airman slid over the bank and into the river. From the high cliff Tien Pao saw him swimming under water. He angled off with the current toward a big branch floating down the middle of the river. The current took him away, and then he was gone from sight. Just the branch floated downriver.

The Japanese had also heard Tien Pao's screams. From across the river up-pointed rifles searched the cliff. A rifle spat. The shot shattered a branch of the thorn bush above Tien Pao's head. Tien Pao shook in terror. Somehow he kept himself from running. One thing he had learned from the airman —he did not run in terror. Instead he threw himself flat and lay still as death behind the bush. He pressed Glory-of-the-Republic down beside him. But he couldn't keep himself from staring in fascinated horror through the branches of the bush at the up-pointed searching rifles. It couldn't be believed! He could clearly see the riflemen with their cheeks laid over the rifles, searching, aiming. Searching for him, aiming for him—to kill him. It couldn't be believed!

Tien Pao had to fight off panic. Had to fight to keep from running headlong over the cliff and down the path. He must keep down, mustn't move; and if he moved, he mustn't raise himself at all, but crawl, slow, slow, slow. That was what the airman had done—slow now, keep down, crawl.

Slowly Tien Pao twisted his face away from the riverbank and the rifles. He studied the path up which he had come. Slow now, slow. Slide flat, inch ahead. Holding Glory-of-the-Republic down by the front legs so he couldn't possibly rear up, Tien Pao slithered face down toward the path up which he had come. He dragged the little pig inch by inch beside him. Glory-of-the-Republic mustn't squirm. No, Glory, no!

The little pig did not care to be dragged along on his side. He grunted, he struggled. Tien Pao forced him down again. Even that quick movement had been seen. A shot rang out. The bullet smashed against the polished boulder, bounced and caromed off with an angry, stinging whine. Something smacked hard against Tien Pao's cheek. He clapped his hand to his stunned cheek. His hand came away bloody.

Before him lay the flattened slug of the bullet that had bounded from the rock and hit his cheek. Tien Pao stared at it—stared at his bloody hand. He lay deathly still. It was suddenly silent down below in the valley. Then there were shouts far down the river. And Tien Pao knew horror, for he realized what the Japanese were doing. They were going after the airman in force, but meanwhile one or two riflemen were keeping him on the high, solitary cliff. That was all that was needed—just a bullet now and then to keep him on the cliff—and when they had the airman, they'd come and get him. There were two shots far downriver.

Much later, out of the stillness in the valley came a scream. A short scream, cut off. Had they caught him? They must have caught the airman! They were torturing him! Now they would come across the river and mount the cliff to capture him and Glory-of-the-Republic. Tien Pao's outstretched hand clenched and unclenched around the bullet slug on the ground before him. He had to know, had to raise his head to see what was happening in the still valley.

A sampan was leaving the opposite bank of the river, a sampan full of soldiers. It was heading straight for the cliff, coming for him! They were coming—they'd torture him, too, for what he had done.

In his terror Tien Pao forgot all caution. He flung himself up, fled headlong over the round top of the cliff. At his first lunge the shots rang out. Tien Pao crazily threw himself ahead of the vicious whistling sound of bullets, threw himself over the round top of the cliff as if he could outrace bullets. Then he was over the cliff. For the moment he was out of range of the riflemen, protected by the shoulder of the cliff. But he tore on at the blind, mad pace down the steep cliff. He fell, picked himself up, raced on again. Glory-of-the-Republic bowled on behind him.

They were at the little cave in which they had spent the night. Without thinking, Tien Pao threw himself flat and started to crawl in. He backed right out again. He couldn't hide here—the Japanese would search every inch of the cliff, every hole and crevice. He had to get far away from this cliff.

They raced on again. They left the lone cliff behind, ran back the way they had come the night before, ran downriver the way the airman had gone. Tien Pao did not know where he was going, but anywhere, anywhere away from the cliff and the bullets—any place was better. Then the thought struck him: if the Japanese had not yet caught the American airman, this whole country downriver would be full of searching parties. He forced himself to slow down, be cautious, listen—he mustn't go crashing along paths to run full tilt into the Japanese. He had to hide at once.

He left the path and edged up the first cliff that looked as if it might provide shelter and concealment. The squat cliff was strewn with huge rocks, and all the tight spaces between the rocks were jammed with brush and thorns. It was terrible, impossible climbing. Glory-of-the-Republic lagged more and more behind. Tien Pao had to wait for him. At the spot where Tien Pao stood waiting, the leaves lay heaped high in the split of a rock. This wasn't a cave, just a narrow crevice open to the sky, but it might be possible to hide behind the high-piled leaves. It would have to do—Glory-of-the-Republic was grunting so painfully, Tien Pao knew he could hardly climb any more. He grabbed a handful of leaves, held them up, crunched and rattled them to coax the little pig on. Then he attacked the piled leaves, raking and pawing them away with both hands to get at the crevice.

Tien Pao stopped for a moment, looked back to see if Glory-of-the-Republic was coming. In the momentary quiet there was a rattling in the leaves not of Tien Pao's making. Swift as a snake, a hand struck through the piled leaves. The hand grabbed Tien Pao's throat. Tien Pao's startled scream was cut off as the savage grip closed around his throat. He was jerked off his feet, head-first into the pile of leaves. In his terror Tien Pao thrashed so fiercely in the leaves, Glory-of-the-Republic became frightened and bolted down the cliff.

In the crevice of the rock Tien Pao's terrified eyes stared at a white, blotched face, singed hair. It was the airman! *His* airman—his river god! The airman did not know him. His grip tightened around Tien Pao's throat, and his other hand clamped over Tien Pao's mouth so hard, Tien Pao's lips crushed down on his teeth. He tasted blood. His eyes started out of their sockets. He felt himself going limp.

Dimly he still heard a rustling among the leaves —as if far away. But the airman whipped around to face whatever was coming. Then Glory-of-the-Republic burst through the piled leaves. The startled airman looked from the pig to the boy he was choking. Immediately he released his hold on Tien Pao. A great gush of air sobbed into Tien Pao's empty lungs. He shook his head to clear his eyes. He managed a sick little smile.

The man grinned back, but he looked terribly puzzled. Then Tien Pao realized that, dirty as he was, thin and starved and caked with paddy mud, the airman had not recognized him. If it hadn't been for Glory-of-the-Republic . . . Tien Pao rubbed his throat, let out his breath in one big, nervous gasp. He knew the airman could not imagine why he and his pig were here. But how could he tell him? Tien Pao pointed up to the sky. Then he made his hand go spiraling down, the way the airplane had gone down. He cupped his hands to his mouth as if shouting a great shout, then pointed to himself. The airman grinned, nodded. He understood!

They sat grinning at each other—they had no words. The airman began building up the disturbed leaf pile again, but Tien Pao leaned back against the rock pile with a great, tired sigh. Now he was safe! He laughed a little, he felt so safe with the airman, even though the Japanese might be all around.

The airman turned to look hard at him. Tien Pao looked back at the airman and laughed and laughed until tears filled his eyes. Then he wasn't laughing, he was crying. Now he was safe, but he was crying, and right before the airman. Tien Pao turned his shamed face away, he grabbed the little pig, and

pulled him to his chest. He tried to muffle the hard, wrenching sobs against the little pig's muddy hide.

Tien Pao did not know that this was shock and the reaction from the terrible danger, now that he was suddenly safe. But the airman knew. He reached over, pushed the pig away, and took Tien Pao into his own lap. He sat and rocked the sobbing Tien Pao, gently, slowly, like a mother. And the airman, in the soft, sweet relief of his own escape from death, crooned like a mother to a little baby: "I know. I know just how you feel, little fellow. You don't have to be ashamed. I know how it feels to be shot at."

Tien Pao did not understand, but the words were soothing, and at last he managed to grin up at the man. At once the airman poked his finger into Tien Pao's hollow stomach. It must mean: "Have you eaten?"

Tien Pao dashed his tears away, and sat up eagerly. He shook his head. He grabbed a leaf and crunched it between his teeth to show what he had been eating. The airman made a face. He began digging in his pockets. Tien Pao could not keep his eyes away from the man's searching hand. At last the airman drew a bar of chocolate from one of his many pockets. He broke off a morsel and gave it to Tien Pao. He started to give Glory-of-the-Republic a tiny piece, but with a wry grin he gave the little pig a handful of leaves instead, and handed the second morsel also to Tien Pao.

Tien Pao kept the second little piece of chocolate pinched between his fingers while he slowly chewed the first little piece. He slowly let it melt in his mouth. He let it trickle around his teeth, and then slowly, oh, very slowly and sweetly, flow down his throat. Never in his life had he tasted anything so heavenly. After it was gone he licked around his lips for any left-over droplet of chocolate. And then there was still the other little piece. Now he could do it all over again—let it melt, let it trickle, let it slide in all its sweetness to his gnawing stomach. He closed his eyes. He rocked himself in the joy of it.

When he opened his eyes, the chocolate was gone. He badly wanted to ask for more. His stomach all but screamed for more, but he did not ask, for he suspected that the one bar of chocolate was all the airman had—one piece to break a crumb from now and then in their days and nights ahead.

Their days and nights ahead! Why, now he wouldn't be alone any more! Tien Pao laughed softly up at the airman. The airman closed his arm around Tien Pao. He understood! It didn't need words.

Together they suddenly tensed, sat up. Down below in the unseen valley the rumble had begun, the grinding sound of trucks came through the wall of leaves. It must mean that the Japanese had abandoned the search, the convoy was on its way again on the road in the valley. They looked at each other and Tien Pao opened his mouth to say something, but the airman laid a finger on his lips. He must mean that it might be a trick, and that they still must be cautious—all the Japanese had not necessarily gone on with the convoy. All the same, Tien Pao and the airman both leaned against the rock wall of the crevice and together they sighed their relief.

The bubbling feeling of wonderful safety was so enormous in him, Tien Pao somehow had to indicate how he felt. Somehow he had to tell the airman that they would go on together. He closed his eyes as if in sleep and pointed to them. That had to indicate the night. He made his fingers walk along his legs, made them climb, made them go down. It had to mean that when night came they would set out through the dark river mountains together.

But the airman looked anxious. First he pulled Tien Pao's face close to him and peered at the wounded cheek. He tossed his head to indicate it looked all right, but then he raised his own trouser leg and showed Tien Pao an ugly gaping wound, an awful, deep, huge burn. The burn already looked poisonous, tinged green-black around the edges. The airman made his fingers walk, pointed to his leg, and shook his head. It meant he could not walk. He groaned and ran the tip of his tongue around his lips—that must mean the wound was making him sick and feverish after the struggle to get to this hideout.

Tien Pao nodded and nodded to show that he completely understood. To further show it, he hastily began making a bed of the leaves. He indicated that the airman should lie down and sleep. He opened his own eyes wide and held them open with his fingers to tell the man that he would keep watch. The man nodded eagerly, stretched out. Almost the next moment he was asleep.

Tien Pao sat beside the airman, hovering over him, watching, ready to lay his hand over the man's mouth, for the airman tossed in an unhappy, feverish sleep, and often he talked out in his foreign tongue. And no one must hear! It was so unbelievably good not to be alone—so good to be with a human being! Nothing must separate them again until they got to Hengyang.

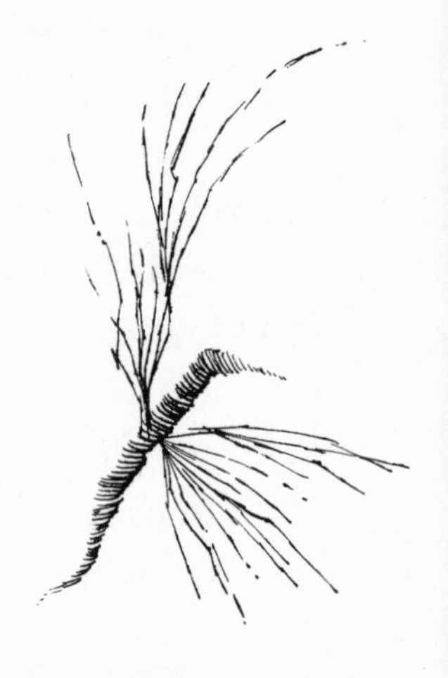

CHAPTER FIVE

CUCKOOS CALL AT NIGHT

They must go on. As soon as it was night, they must go on. Wounded and sick and feverish as the American was, somehow he had to walk. It was not safe to stay in the same place too long. With a stiff grimace the airman agreed. They had held a conference, Tien Pao and the American—a conference without words—and they had agreed that in spite of the wound in the awful, swollen, black leg, they would have to move on. At the very least he would have to limp to another hiding-place, but if at all possible they would walk all night. Perhaps it would be better to rest the leg another day and night, but it was impossible to tell; the wound might become so bad that the airman would not be able to move at all. And they had to move! If the Japanese were still searching, it wasn't safe to stay in one place—sooner or later they'd find it!

When the gathering shadows lay long down the mountains, Tien Pao got ready to leave the cave to find water. The airman needed water. He was burning up, his lips were cracking. When toward evening the man briefly roused from his tossing, restless sleep, Tien Pao picked up the leather helmet to indicate to him that he was going after water. The airman ran his hot tongue over his cracked lips and nodded eagerly—he looked greedily at the flat dangling helmet! But he also looked anxious, and he tried to make Tien Pao understand that he must be very careful.

Tien Pao knotted the rope around Glory-of-the-Republic's leg. He made the man hold the other end of the rope. He did it because Glory-of-the-Republic would be sure to set up a struggle to follow him, and that would keep the airman awake. The airman had to stay awake, for in his sleep he talked loud and long in his foreign tongue. Just one word of that foreign language would be a dead giveaway to anyone who heard it. Tien Pao closed the airman's fingers around Glory-of-the-Republic's snout so the little pig couldn't squeal. Then he left.

Outside he listened long. Then he carefully built up the screen of leaves again into a natural-looking heap. It wasn't quite dark, but Tien Pao kept to the shadows of the rocks and brush. He did not dare go down to the river, and the only other place he knew to go for water was the little wet cave in the cliff in which he had hidden.

When Tien Pao at last reached the little cave he saw at once that it had been disturbed. The Japanese had searched it! Tien Pao crawled in, but while he sat crouched in the little hole, waiting for the slow trickle to fill the leather helmet, he suddenly heard voices. He sat still as death, not daring to move, not even daring to breathe. Two Japanese soldiers marched past the cave. They did not stop, they did not stoop to look in—these men must have been the ones who had searched the cave earlier. They passed on, their footsteps faded.

Long after the helmet had filled, Tien Pao still waited. He drank his fill, and then he let the trickle slowly fill the helmet again. It gave him something to do, and he had to force himself to wait—it was almost impossible in his desperate anxiety. The airman might have gone to sleep in the long wait and talked out in his strange voice. Glory-of-the-Republic might have struggled and squealed and broken away. They didn't know that the Japanese were still in these mountains. The larger convoy might have gone on, but a detachment must have been left behind to comb all the area.

At last it was dark enough so that Tien Pao dared venture out of the little cave. He did not dare use the path. He crept along, guarding the precious water and searching out the best possible path among the rocks on the thorn-tight cliffs. He mustn't stumble. Near their hideout Tien Pao sat long in the deep shadows, watching and listening. He was rewarded. A second searching party passed below. Just beyond the squat cliff where Tien Pao sat, he saw the second searching party join the two men who had passed the little watery cave. They marched off together, and Tien Pao guessed that the search might have been called off for the night.

The anxious airman was sitting bolt upright behind the wall of leaves. He had Glory-of-the-Republic clenched in his arms. His face broke into a big relieved grin when he saw Tien Pao worming through the leaves. He grabbed the helmet, he emptied it in gulps. But while the airman drank, Tien Pao had news, bad news. He made believe he was holding a rifle to show that he was telling about the Japanese. He ducked his head and poked it toward every cranny in the crevice to show that Japanese soldiers with rifles were searching everywhere for them. He cradled head in hand and closed his eyes and made his fingers march to show that the

Japanese had gone away for the night. But then he made his fingers walk again and pointed to himself and the airman.

The airman nodded. He pulled his trouser leg down over his wound, he gritted his teeth to show Tien Pao he'd try it. Then he sat listening long. At last he made a motion to Tien Pao, and crawled outside. Tien Pao grabbed Glory-of-the-Republic's rope and crawled out behind him.

It was the first night that Tien Pao was not alone, but in many ways it was the most horrible night of Tien Pao's long journey. At first Tien Pao walked slowly ahead of the man to find the easiest paths for him. They dragged down the first scrubby, rock-strewn hill, and dragged up the next one. The going down was the same slow painful crawl as the going up—every step on the uneven dark path was agony to the wounded man. At times Tien Pao could hear him grind his teeth.

When the path at last widened, Tien Pao began to walk beside the silent airman to give him support. He placed the rope in the man's hand so that Glory-of-the-Republic would help tug him on. They went on again, but at times the man dug his hand so hard into Tien Pao's shoulder, Tien Pao had all he could do to keep from yelping with the pain.

The night wore on, the hours passed, but it seemed to Tien Pao that if he looked back he would still be able to see the split rock where they had spent the day. They stopped again. The airman clutched Tien Pao's shoulder for support. The cold sweat of pain rolled over his face, but he gave Tien Pao a queer, twisted grin, and took up the slow journey again.

At last it came. The tall man reeled on the path. He turned completely around, took an uneven step as if he were hurrying back, and crashed down over Tien Pao. Tien Pao went down under him. He wriggled frantically to worm himself from under the heavy, motionless man. There the big man lay, sprawled across the path. Tien Pao stood over him, shivering with dread. He did not know what to do. Then in the awful silence he heard the murmur of the river far below. Grabbing the airman's helmet, Tien Pao plunged down to the river. Glory-of-the-Republic bowled along at his heels.

Tien Pao hurried back as fast as he could, fearing every moment he would stumble in the blackness of the rocky hillside and spill the precious water. Suddenly he stood stock still. He imagined he'd heard movements, soft voices on top of the hill. Tien Pao went cold with dread. Had the Japanese stumbled across the helpless airman? Then on top of the hill a cuckoo called. Tien Pao's fears eased. The mountain cuckoo had called again. The cuckoo had called. It was a good omen. Tien Pao trotted up the path.

Again a cuckoo called close to Tien Pao, immediately another sleepy cuckoo up the mountain answered him. It was wonderful—the little mountain was full of cuckoos. Oh, everything had to be all right! Tien Pao reached the path and the still figure of the American sprawled across it. No Japanese had found him! Feeling brave and hopeful, Tien Pao dashed the helmetful of water into the airman's still face. He dropped to his knees, waiting for the first breath.

From behind a tall bush at the side of the path stepped a man. Tien Pao heard the soft step. He jumped to his feet, froze there. He had heard but one soft step, but he and the airman and the little pig were inside a ring of armed men. The airman stirred and moaned, but he did not know what was going on.

A tall, bearded man, who must be the leader, pointed with his gun to the airman. "Who is he? And what are you doing with him?" he asked in Chinese.

Tien Pao opened his mouth, but no sound would come. Fear choked his throat. He stood staring down at the helpless figure of the airman. What must he say? Anything he said might be all wrong. It must be best to tell the truth. Tien Pao looked up from the airman to the bearded man, and somehow he found courage and words, and when he began

he talked as he never had talked in his life. He told about the battle he had seen from the high cliff, and that this was the airman who had killed all the Japanese on the road. He told how he had called out a warning from the cliff. The men listened silently. At last the leader nodded. "You have spoken the truth. We, too, know of the great battle of this brave warrior, but we marvel that you found him. We could not find him, nor could we find you."

"It is more that he found me," Tien Pao said hastily. And then he looked earnestly up at the man. "Please, my lord," he begged. "Please, Sir Bandit, do not kill him, for this warrior airman has greatly helped our people."

The men chuckled, the leader stroked his beard in amusement. "Ah, we may look like it, but we are not bandits. We, too, fight the Japanese. We are the Chinese guerrillas of the mountains. We come out at night to kill and destroy the Japanese. But we shall do well by you and the airman."

To Tien Pao's astonishment, the leader made the soft cuckoo call. Down the path there was an answering sleepy call. Two men came silently through the dark; between them they carried a rough, hurriedly made stretcher. Without a word they laid the feverish, muttering airman on the stretcher and trotted off down the path. Some of the guerrilla band went with the stretcher-carriers as guards, but the airman knew nothing of what was happening to him.

After the airman was gone, the leader took Tien Pao on his shoulder. "The pace we set, and the shape you're in—we'll do it this way." When Tien Pao looked back, a guerrilla trotted on behind with Glory-of-the-Republic under his arm as if he weighed no more than a chicken. They set off through the night, deeper into the dark mountains, away from the guiding sound of the river.

The guerrillas moved swiftly and silently through the black mountains, down beaten paths, but also over many secret trails that must be known only to them. They walked as surely as if it had been daylight. No one spoke a word. Tien Pao still marveled at the sudden happening. "Often I heard the sleepy cuckoo call these many nights, but I didn't know," he whispered down to the guerrilla.

The guerrilla chuckled. "We are in all the mountains," he said softly. But then he laid a warning finger on his lips. They were going down a broad, well-worn mountain path—Tien Pao was to talk no more. The guerrilla who was carrying Glory-of-the-Republic had one hand around the little pig's snout. Glory-of-the-Republic was sound asleep. His ears hung limp.

Suddenly there was the hushed cuckoo call. The little procession melted from the path and into the shadows of the rocks. In one moment the trail lay empty, except for the man with Glory-of-the-Republic. Now he set the little pig down in the middle of the path, gave the sleepy pig a sharp, mean jab, and then he was gone from the path, too. Glory-of-the-Republic let out a long, loud squeal. Bewildered and alone, the little pig stood on the path. He raised his nose to snuffle for Tien Pao. He grunted a sharp question.

Down the steep path a Japanese soldier came stealing, gun in hand. For a moment the bayonet on his gun flashed in the dark as he lunged at the unsuspecting little pig. The guerrilla leader clamped a hand over Tien Pao's mouth to keep him still. Tien Pao struggled. But as the leader held him hard, guerrillas slid out of the shadows behind and to either side of the charging Japanese. Suddenly the Japanese soldier charged no more. A black cloth came down from nowhere over his head. Strong hands pinioned his arms. There was a muffled scream, the gun clattered to the rocky path. It bounced up and landed beside the startled little pig.

One muffled, short scream and then the Japanese had vanished down the mountain between two guerrillas. The remaining guerrillas took up the march again. They were silent. Ahead walked the scouts. Far behind, trailing along, each man by himself, came the rear guard. Thus they were protected on all sides from any surprise by the Japanese. But the rest of the night they did not meet a single living thing. Nor did the cuckoo call again.

Toward morning the party at last halted. A little mud house loomed up; it clung to the side of a cliff. There was no one in the little house but an old, withered, toothless crone. At a word from the leader she silently began cooking rice over a ready fire. Tien Pao looked around the little room crowded with the men. "But the airman, where is he?" he demanded wildly. "Where is the American?" Nobody answered. Only the old crone looked at him. The guerrillas were gathered close together, whispering.

Tien Pao was bewildered. "But where then is the Japanese soldier?" he asked in confusion. "Did you kill him?"

"Oh, no. Oh, no," the guerrilla chief said at last. He was mightily pleased with the work of the night. He was examining the rifle taken from the Japanese. "It is a good gun," he said. He ran his fingers over the ammunition belt. It was full except for one bullet. The soldier had evidently intended that for Glory-of-the-Republic, if he couldn't run the little pig through with the silent bayonet. "Oh, no," the chief said. "If we had wanted to kill the Jap, we wouldn't have tricked him with your pig. Alive he is worth far more, alive we can question him."

"But where is the airman?" Tien Pao asked again.

"Not here," the leader said briefly. It was clear he did not want to answer the question.

"What did you do with him?" Tien Pao persisted. "I must know. He is my friend."

The guerrilla shook his head. "Your white friend is safe, that is all you need to know," he told Tien Pao. "And do not ask any more. It is far better that you do not know how we are taking him back to the American lines. You are still more than a day's journey inside Japanese territory, and you might still be captured. And then you would talk. Oh, yes, you would talk! But if you do not know, you cannot tell."

Tien Pao nodded somberly. The words filled him with sick horror. But the food had begun cooking, and Tien Pao forgot everything for the heavenly odors of the rice and greens. He almost fainted over the bowl of steaming rice that was handed to him. All the men were hungry. They ate hurriedly and silently. Tien Pao wolfed his bowlful. He was holding out his bowl for more when at a whispered word from the leader the men arose. The journey was to go on even by day. The guerrillas wanted to get Tien Pao out of Japanese country as fast as the airman. They knew only too bitterly well what happened to those who helped American pilots to escape.

At a nod from the leader, the old woman went to a secret hole in the wall and took out buckets and carrying-poles and hoes. Tien Pao was to carry two buckets. "Now remember this," the guerrilla chief told him, "during the day we do not fight the Japanese. We are now farmers. If we meet Japanese on the path, do not run, no matter how scared you may be. When the warning comes, get off the path as soon as possible and go to the nearest rice paddy with your buckets. But do not run! Act exactly as if it were your father's rice paddy. Do you understand?

"Another thing," the leader said. "Today I am your father, Huan. You will trot at a respectable distance behind me with your buckets. Your name is Tsu, and you are not too bright. If we are questioned by the Japanese, let me do the talking. If they speak to you directly, act the fool, and don't be alarmed if I abuse you and even slap your face for your stupid answers. Now repeat our names, and remember them."

Tien Pao repeated the names.

"One more thing," the guerrilla said, "if any of the Japanese that pass us order you to work—work for them. Do not show that you hate them, work for them willingly—it is at night that we kill them."

One of the guerrillas had fitted a false bottom with air holes into one of Tien Pao's buckets. Glory-of-the-Republic had been trussed up, legs and snout. The old woman had brought a little pile of old, wet straw and litter. Now Glory-of-the-Republic was lowered into the bucket, the false bottom was pounded over him, and the rubbish and straw were spread over the false bottom. The second bucket was filled with heavier litter. The buckets were now balanced on the carrying-pole, and both looked equally full and heavy. It was hard to see Glory-of-the-Republic trussed up and shoved into the bottom of a bucket, but Tien Pao realized they could not travel by day in Japanese-occupied territory with a pig.

"Son, Tsu, we must go," the guerrilla leader ordered. He threw a hoe over his shoulder.

"Ready, honorable father, Huan," Tien Pao said meekly. He braced his shoulders under the carrying-pole and started to lift the buckets.

"A moment, please," the old crone mumbled apologetically to the guerrilla leader. With a toothless smile for Tien Pao she hastily brought him a second bowl of rice.

The guerrilla impatiently lowered his hoe, but he said nothing.

"Because of the heavy load and the starved lad—the journey will go much better for a second bowl of rice," she apologized. "A child must eat. And . . . and I love a child."

The guerrilla smiled a little, and Tien Pao hastily wolfed the rice. "Ready," he said with his mouth full of food, and shouldered his loaded buckets. He trotted out behind his so-called father. But outside the door he turned, and said with all his heart to the old crone: "And I love you."

It was a lovely smile her old mouth gave him in their parting.

"Aren't the others coming?" Tien Pao asked, puzzled, after he and the guerrilla leader had been on the trail awhile.

"In the daytime we do not travel in groups—each

man is on his own. It is best also that you do not follow so closely at my heels. Keep at a distance," the guerrilla ordered.

Tien Pao fell back. He trotted at a distance behind the leader all that morning. They gave no sign that they knew each other. At noon the guerilla had a warning that a small detachment of Japanese cavalry was on the mountain path. Tien Pao's so-called father hurried to a nearby rice paddy and wearily began turning clods as if he had been working at it since early dawn. Tien Pao became confused; he dreaded meeting the Japanese alone, but he did not know whether he was to join the guerrilla or find a paddy of his own. He trotted up the path as fast as he could in the hope that he'd find another rice paddy over the hill.

Over the rise burst a file of Japanese horsemen. They galloped straight down on Tien Pao. Tien Pao's heart fluttered. He wanted to run, but he crowded to the side of the path and kept jogging along under his loaded buckets. To his relief, the Japanese horsemen passed him without so much as a glance at him. Then one of the buckets happened to graze the leg of an officer's pony. The horse shied. The officer had him under control in a moment, but instead of riding on, he whipped his pony around on the path and charged him straight at Tien Pao.

There was nothing to do. Tien Pao flung himself over the bucket in which Glory-of-the-Republic was hidden. Above him reared the horse, hoofs pawing the air. But the horse was afraid of the sprawled Tien Pao. Snorting with fear, it backed away on its hind legs. With a curse the officer rammed his spurs into the animal's flanks. But instead of coming down on Tien Pao, the trembling horse in one wild plunge cleared Tien Pao, buckets and all, and tore headlong down the steep, rocky side of the hill.

There had been no time for fear, but now that officer and horse were gone, Tien Pao began shaking all over, weeping from rage and hate. A second, bigger detachment of Japanese came over the hill, but Tien Pao, standing between his buckets, weeping out his rage, did not notice, and when they were on top of him, he was too unnerved to move.

The guerrilla in the rice paddy had seen what was happening to Tien Pao, and came running. "Here, stupid son," he shouted angrily. "Here, fool, weakling, lazy oaf—the manure must be here that my paddy may sprout the rice of a good harvest for us and our Japanese friends. And it doesn't need watering with your tears!" He came running with the hoe as if he would like to break it over Tien Pao's head. The passing Japanese laughed among themselves at the comical scene made by the two stupid Chinese farmers.

The guerrilla took Tien Pao by the shoulders and shook him violently, but under his breath he said: "It is well. Don't lose your head now, you did so well."

That was all he said, but, encouraged, Tien Pao took up the buckets. The journey went on again.

Tien Pao was bone-tired and tottering when in the late afternoon they entered a house. Rice was steaming, and the odor of good food so filled the house that Tien Pao became weak and dazed. He fumbled clumsily with the bucket to let Glory-of-the-Republic out of his cramped quarters. A young woman took the bucket from him, and handed him a bowl of steaming rice instead. Tien Pao did not even look up at her, just sat stooped over his rice, letting the steam from the beautiful big white kernels curl up around his nose.

There were no guerrillas here. There was no one in the house but the young woman. The guerrilla leader turned to Tien Pao. "This is your mother while we are here. This is my wife—Yin."

Tien Pao started—it was the exact name of his own mother! The pretty young woman even looked like his mother! Tien Pao sat staring at her, and such longing rose in him for his own mother, his hunger almost left him. The young woman, who was feeding Glory-of-the-Republic, saw him staring. She smiled and nodded for him to start eating. She understood! Tien Pao ate, but his heart was full.

Suddenly the guerrilla chief asked the young woman: "Was a beggar carried past the house here?"

She nodded. "Oh, hours ago, and if they keep on at the pace they were going, the beggar should be in friendly territory by the time night falls."

Tien Pao was puzzled, but suddenly Yin laughed and said: "Oh, it worked splendidly! One man was carrying the old graybeard piggy-back. And that old beggar looked so piteous, even a Japanese officer dropped some small money in the wooden bowl the beggar held in his dirty hand. Immediately afterwards he became so furious with himself for his moment of weakness, I was told, that from then on he pushed everybody and everything out of his path."

Tien Pao laughed with the young woman, who did not see her husband's warning glance. "I wonder if that was the same cavalry officer who tried to run me down with his horse."

The guerrilla had to tell the story to Yin.

"Charge a horse at a boy, and let an American airman pass under his nose," Yin said contemptuously.

Then it struck Tien Pao. "But if the airman will soon be safe, why, then I'll soon be in friendly territory, too!" he exclaimed.

"A few more hours of walking tomorrow morning, and you'll be out of the Japanese lines," the guerrilla assured him. "Just a few more hours of hoeing and manuring your father's rice paddies, and you'll be safe. But understand, your father has many rice paddies all over China, and he hoes and manures them well with his oaf of a son."

They laughed. They ate a hearty meal with laughter. Then the guerrilla left on some secret errand of his own.

"A few more hours," Tien Pao marveled aloud after the meal was over. He still couldn't believe it. It seemed almost impossible after the many long days and longer nights—a few more hours in the morning.

"Just a few more hours, really!" the young woman said gaily.

"But then why can't we go right on, like the airman?"

Yin shook her head. "Your so-called father has other things to do this night. And then the wounded airman is being carried, but after the beating you've been taking all these days and nights, and no food—you couldn't keep it up with those heavy buckets. . . . Ah, but you need a bath."

The young woman hauled out a wooden tub and splashed warm water into it. Tien Pao began taking off his mud-caked clothes, but they wouldn't

come, they stuck. He had to ask Yin to help—it hurt too much. Yin soaked them loose, but she looked thoughtful and serious when the cloth stuck in old wounds, and she winced with Tien Pao when she worked the stuck cloth loose. When Tien Pao was finally stripped, Yin vigorously scrubbed his dirt, but she daubed gently at his many sores and bruises, and muttered angrily to herself whenever she hurt him.

"After you've bathed me, may I bathe Glory-of-the-Republic in the tub?" Tien Pao asked. "He's a very proper pig, and he has many wounds, too—

it's pretty hard to stay on your feet, climbing mountains in the dark."

The guerrilla leader, coming into the house, heard Tien Pao's plea for Glory-of-the-Republic. "Oh, so," he said, "is that the name of your pig! Well, it's a good name, for we're going to have much use for him in fighting for the republic. He tricked one Jap, and he's going to trick more. They just love pork! They can't resist it when they hear it squealing on some dark mountain path."

The guerrilla laughed, but Tien Pao did not laugh. "Glory-of-the-Republic is all I have," he said softly.

"In that you have more than we," the guerrilla said sternly. "We half starve while we work for the Japanese. We fight them at night, and they hunt us night and day. You remember the old crone who gave you that second bowl of rice this morning?"

"Oh, I do," Tien Pao said fervently.

"Well, word has just come to me—the Japanese burned her house, and she was in it. And you don't even want to sacrifice a pig!"

Tien Pao paled, and he did not know what to say after that awful news. . . . Any way he said it, it would sound selfish and hard-hearted. He finally said it to the young woman, but he did not dare look at the guerrilla. "I have lost my home, the sampan, and the ducklings," he almost whispered. "Nor do I know if I will ever get back to my father and mother and my baby sister. The little pig was all I had in the dark nights in the mountains, and I was not so brave, but I had Glory-of-the-Republic."

"Brave!" the young woman declared flatly. Then she held Tien Pao at arm's length, turned him around and around so that the guerrilla chief could see every part of his body. "Look at him! Look at that, and that, and that! Battered and bruised all over his body. And you want to take his pig from him to catch one more miserable Jap! It's not for me to dispute your decisions—but didn't he save the airman's life?"

The guerrilla smiled. "What can a man do against a woman and a child? It is well, my son. You've been a fine young warrior for China. The pig is yours. . . . And now I'm going to bed for a few hours' sleep."

But Tien Pao swooped at Glory-of-the-Republic, threw him into the tub, and washed him so splashily that it made a racket. But it was all done so that they could not hear that he was crying. And he was secretly relieved when the guerrilla chief went to bed.

That night Glory-of-the-Republic slept in a secret place inside a double wall of the house, but after the guerrilla left on his night mission, Tien Pao slept in the bed with his so-called mother. It was soft, it was warm; it was glorious and safe. And the young woman held him close.

CHAPTER SIX

IN THE TOWN OF TERROR

Early the next morning Tien Pao and the guerrilla chief began the last day's journey. The guerrilla urged Tien Pao on, but Tien Pao turned once more to wave still another last farewell to the young woman in the doorway.

"You won't get to Hengyang walking backward," the guerrilla said. "It's still a full day's march."

"Are you going to take me all the way?" Tien Pao asked. He shifted the carrying-pole to a more secure position on his shoulder. Glory-of-the-Republic was back in the bucket. The buckets already seemed heavy, and his shoulder was still sore from yesterday's jogging and constant sawing of the pole. It felt as if the jiggling pole had ground down to the bone.

"No, not all the way, but I'll get you well beyond the Japanese lines. We should manage that by noon, and from there on you should be able to see the town from the mountaintops. . . . Now no more talk. Fall back and follow me at a distance again."

All that day they did not pass a single Japanese. Gradually the guerrilla led Tien Pao back to the river, so that Tien Pao could follow it to Hengyang when he had to go on alone. But as they neared the river, they neared the Japanese. There at last was the river, and there again the road in the valley beyond the river. On the road were the same heavy rumble of trucks and the hoofbeats of cavalry that Tien Pao had heard during his long nights in the mountains. But here also was the steady tread of marching soldiers. The Japanese were on the march in force.

Tien Pao and the guerrilla stood looking down on it all. "Fast as we traveled," the man muttered, "they traveled faster. It's a forced march, and that can mean only one thing—they're out to take the city."

"Hengyang?" Tien Pao asked fearfully.

Together they stood on the peak of a high river mountain. The guerrilla did not answer, just stood looking somberly into the far distance. Tien Pao let down the heavy buckets and stared where the man was staring. In a faraway bend of the river lay a distant town. From the town came a vague rumble as of thunder. Smoke rose from the town.

"Hengyang?" Tien Pao asked again.

The guerrilla nodded. "That is Hengyang, the town you started from, but now I can take you no farther. I promised to take you beyond the Japanese lines, but those turned out to be foolish words—the Japanese are already at the gates of Hengyang. When you go on alone, keep to the mountains and walk beyond the town, then circle down and enter it by the street of the rear gate—the river's not far from that gate."

"But Hengyang is on fire!"

"Still it cannot be all destroyed," the man said somberly. "I just now saw the flash of guns coming out of the town. That means our armies are still battling for it."

"But would my mother and father still be in such a town of battle?"

The guerrilla smiled a thin smile. "If I know a father, he will wait until the last moment in the small hope that you may return. And if I know a mother, she will wait until the Japanese are in the streets and their bayonets at her back before she gives up a firstborn son."

Tien Pao nodded eagerly along with the words, but the picture of his mother with Japanese bayonets at her back filled him with sudden, overpowering dread. He hoisted the pole and buckets to his shoulder. "But then I have to go," he said anxiously. "Then I have to hurry. I have to go."

The guerrilla chief laid his hand on Tien Pao's shoulder. "And may it go well with you, son."

"May it go well with you," Tien Pao mumbled. He set off at an anxious trot. Later he turned. He had not even thanked the guerrilla for all he had done! But the guerrilla chief was gone from sight over the mountain. Tien Pao stood rubbing his aching shoulder, staring back along the empty mountain path. With a heavy sigh he took up his buckets and trotted off toward the smoke clouds over the distant town. So they parted.

The tall mountain from which he and the guerrilla chief had first seen Hengyang had fooled Tien Pao. He walked for hours, but still the town and its billowing smoke looked no nearer; only the boom of the cannon echoed louder among the high rocks. The afternoon waned and the evening came and Tien Pao was still in the mountains. The carrying-pole cut into his flesh as he struggled on. For the hundredth time he shifted the pole and its load to the other shoulder. A weird glow from the burning town hung in the sky; the red glow spread as the mountains began to gather night darkness. Wearily Tien Pao stumbled on.

It was almost midnight when Tien Pao reached Hengyang by the street of the rear gate. No sentry in the gate challenged him. No hurrying Chinese soldier looked at him. But in the narrow street a mass of people surging toward the gate knocked Tien Pao down.

Tien Pao picked himself up, too numb with weariness to care or understand. People were running in the night. They ran by him, bent under bundles and straining at heavy carts loaded with household goods. They wheeled by in rickshaws almost buried under their household belongings. The wheels of rickshaws grazed Tien Pao. Everybody was running out of the town, only Tien Pao went into the town. He stumbled under the weight of his buckets. The surge of the crowd pushed him to the side of the street into the shadows of the buildings. Nobody noticed him.

At the far end of the town were the thunder of guns and the swift white flashes. Flames leaped over the roofs. Smoke billowed black above the shooting flames. Tien Pao dragged himself on, too stupid with weariness to hear or see what went on around him. People yelled and people wept. Mothers called frantically to keep their children

near them in the surge of the milling crowd. Fathers tried to herd their families together. Everybody was running. Tien Pao was pushed into the doorway of a building.

Tien Pao leaned heavily against the shadowy building to rest for a few moments. He let himself sag until he sat on one of the buckets. Almost immediately his head began to nod. The rolling boom of the cannon jerked him awake again. He staggered on, deeper into the town, closer to the sound of battle and the hot roar of the fire. But where was the river?

At last Tien Pao could carry his burden no longer. He stopped and spilled the litter out of the one bucket, pulled out the false bottom, and lifted out the trussed-up little pig. He fumblingly undid the ropes that bound Glory-of-the-Republic, and knotted them together to make a short leash. The little pig, weary of his cramped quarters, trotted eagerly ahead. He tugged Tien Pao along by the rope.

"Maybe you know where the river is," Tien Pao mumbled hopelessly. "Maybe you can smell it. The people are running and the sky is on fire, and I don't know anything any more." He let the little pig pull him.

Glory-of-the-Republic stopped to snuffle and snort among some garbage under an arch. Tien Pao let himself sag against the base of the arch. The dark mass of people streamed by. Suddenly an old woman with a deep, hamper-like basket strapped to her back darted out of the crowd. She grabbed the rope in Tien Pao's hand. As if he had been hit by one of the stray bullets whistling overhead, Tien Pao jumped up. He looked wildly at the old woman. "It is my pig," he said thickly. "He is mine, let go of the rope."

The old hag kept tugging. "You are taking him to the Japanese!" she screamed. "I saw you—you were going to the end of town where the Japanese are. And I, I die of hunger."

"The Japanese aren't in the town," Tien Pao yelled back. He wouldn't believe it.

"Don't you see the people running? Even our soldiers are running. Hengyang is falling. Our army is defeated."

Tien Pao looked toward the burning part of the town. Flames shot high among tall buildings. By the light of the flames Tien Pao saw swift planes high in the sky There was the heavy, ominous sound of bombs exploding.

"Where is the river?" Tien Pao yelled.

"Why, right behind the houses of this next street. But there's no safety in the river. All the sampans are gone, and . . ."

Tien Pao lunged and gave the old woman such a savage shove, she toppled backward over her basket, but she still clung to the rope. Tien Pao jerked the rope from her hand, let his buckets stand, and with his little pig raced madly toward the river.

There was the river! At last, at last. Tien Pao tore along it. There at last was the path that had led to the sampans. And there was the steep bank where their sampan had lain. But the river was empty! There were no sampans! There was not one sampan left of the whole row of sampans.

Tien Pao sank down on the bank. Behind him in all the streets was the scurrying noise of running feet, the shouting and the running. They were gone—his father and mother. They had not waited for him. But he had never thought—how could his father and mother have been waiting at the river? They could not have bought another sampan—they had no money. Most likely they had gone into the city to live in some hut. But where was he to find them in all the crooked streets? He did not know the town. . . . And maybe with the Japanese attacking they had already left Hengyang. Maybe even now they were running before the Japanese with all the others. Perhaps they had passed him in the crowds. Perhaps, perhaps . . . maybe, maybe . . . but a thousand things could have happened! Tien Pao gave up his agonized guessing and stared dully at the river.

Where the town was burning, the river was blood-red from the glare of the flames. Whole houses crashed. As Tien Pao looked, the front of a three-story building collapsed into the water among a roar of flames and a seething hiss of steam. Among the smoldering beams and crackling wreckage an empty sampan came drifting toward Tien Pao. It burst into flames from the heat on the river. Flaming like a great torch, it drifted past. Tien Pao could stand no more. He jumped to his feet and turned to run.

Behind him stood the hag!

She had her insane, beady eyes on him. "So your father and mother left you behind to shift for yourself," she cackled.

Tien Pao nodded dumbly.

"Then come with me, for I am a sick old woman, and my family, too, left me behind to die."

Tien Pao did not trust her shifty eyes. She still wanted to steal Glory-of-the-Republic. He held the rope tighter, but he did not know what else to do.

Hopelessly he looked up at the insane old woman. In the street beyond them there was the hard, measured running of whole troops of soldiers.

"Listen," the old woman said, "now even our soldiers are running away." She grabbed Tien Pao's hand, and he let himself be dragged along. He did not care any more what happened to him. The old woman suddenly stopped, took down her deep, hamper-like basket, ripped the rope from Tien Pao's hand, and was going to dump the little pig into the basket. At that Tien Pao fought her. He grabbed up Glory-of-the-Republic and would not let her touch him.

"Listen," the hag said, "you can carry the basket with your precious pig, but we've got to hide him. Hengyang is starved, they'd steal him." Suddenly she tipped the basket upside down. Out of the bottom rolled a thick, tied-up bundle of money. She scooped it up and shook it in Tien Pao's face. "Look, I have plenty of money for tickets to get on the train. It's our only chance. We'll fool our families! They left us behind to die, so we'll save ourselves. You'll be my family now."

She was crazy!

"I found the money," she whispered secretively in Tien Pao's ear. Her high, queer laugh cackled out again.

She'd stolen the money! Tien Pao did not care,

did not care about anything now—except Glory-of-the-Republic. He himself lowered the little pig to the bottom of the basket; only then did he let the woman hang the basket over his shoulders and drag him on, he didn't care where.

The beggar woman seemed to know every inch of the town. She hurried Tien Pao along alleys and down narrow dark passageways under buildings. Although she was old, she was wiry, and she ran like a frightened calf. Panting and gasping, they emerged from an alley and stood before a huge stone building. Beyond the gloomy building stood locomotives with long trains of cars behind them. The cars were almost hidden by the mobs of people milling around them. All the cars swarmed with people. They crowded every inch of every roof, they squeezed out of doorways and open windows. Men, women, and children lay under the trains between the enormous wheels. People even clung to the steely sides of the locomotives. And still more people stormed the standing trains.

A heavy iron gate separated Tien Pao and the beggar woman from the railyard where the trains stood puffing. The old woman forced her way through the packed mass of people at the gate, she thrust a thick bundle of money at a man in uniform. The man grabbed the money. As if by magic the gate drew open, but only wide enough to let Tien

Pao and the old woman squeeze through. Behind them the howling crowd surged forward, but soldiers with bayonets forced the mob back. Only those who had money, it seemed, could save themselves.

Inside the gate, Tien Pao was almost lifted off his feet by the mob surging around the trains. The old woman shrieked and used her elbows. She had no shame. She even elbowed men out of her way. And if she had to, she got down on hands and knees and crawled between the legs of men. But whenever the basket with Glory-of-the-Republic got in Tien Pao's way so he could not follow her, she waited for Tien Pao, or made room for him. "Hang on to me. Follow me," she ordered shrilly. Ranting, spitting, screaming, she forced herself a path. Tien Pao clung to her torn, dirty jacket.

They reached the passenger train. There was no room for so much as a mouse on the whole train. When she saw that, the old woman let out an insane scream. She cursed and spat and tore her thin hair. Tien Pao backed away from her. She was mad. Mad!

"There is still room in the freight train," a voice in the crowd shouted. In a moment Tien Pao was lifted off his feet and swept away from the old woman. He was swept along in the crush of the crowd that stampeded toward the freight train on a farther track. He was carried along, his feet hardly touching ground. His basket was almost torn from his back, the straps cut into his shoulders. As if he had been washed by a tide, he felt himself thrown up toward the open doorway of one of the freight cars. For a moment he saw the high doorway before him, then he was heaved by the crowd's surge under the train and against one of the huge iron wheels. He clawed himself up by the rim of the wheel. Glory-of-the-Republic grunted in the basket.

It was hopeless. The freight car was as packed as the passenger train. Even the wide doorway was solid with people. They teetered on the edge. Tien Pao clung to the wheel to keep himself from being crushed. Hopelessly he looked up at the high doorway. For a moment a tall soldier standing in the doorway looked down in his eyes. Suddenly he stooped, his long arm shot out; he grabbed Tien Pao's collar and lifted him into the car like a drowned puppy. But the press of the crowd inside the boxcar was so great, Tien Pao could do no more than get a toehold on the edge of the doorway. He clung to the soldier's leg.

The man turned on the people behind him. "There must be room for one thin, starved boy," he said savagely. "Stand back. Back! Or I'll make room."

The people were packed in a solid mass, but somehow they made room. Tien Pao could edge into the doorway, but the basket on his back hung outside. There was nothing to be done about it. Without warning, the freight train suddenly lurched into motion. The people on the ground went mad. They flung themselves up at the moving doorway, but the long-armed soldier, without a muscle moving in his face, flung them back as fast as they came. Tien Pao clung to his leg.

At last the soldier looked at him. "Because you reminded me of my firstborn I left behind seven years ago in my house by the sea, I saved you." Then he noticed the basket. "Throw that away," he said harshly. "There's no room." He grabbed the straps and jerked them down Tien Pao's arms.

"Please, soldier," Tien Pao begged. "My pig is in there." He looked anxiously at the massed people. "Now you'll want to eat him, but he saved an American airman from the Japanese," he said desperately, "and he is all I have."

"Oh, ho, and is it so!" the soldier laughed. "Saved an airman, eh? Then into the basket with you, too. That way you won't take extra room. Don't worry, I'll guard it." He lifted Tien Pao into the deep basket. He turned and struck the leather holster of his huge pistol. "None of you want to eat pig, do you?"

No one answered a word. The train had stopped! For no seeming reason the freight train had stopped

—now instead the passenger train began chugging into motion on the other track. Tien Pao saw the beggar woman the moment the passenger train began rolling. There she was, clinging to the side of a car, pulling herself in through a window. Hands reached out and dragged at her, but evidently there was no room, and there she hung, half through the window, half out. The shameless, mad hag had got on the passenger train after all.

Now with the passenger train moving alongside on the other track, Tien Pao's freight train began jolting and jerking again. But at that moment there came the sudden hard clatter of rifle fire. Bullets shrieked and whistled along the train. One slammed overhead into the thick wooden wall of the boxcar. Now the soldiers who had guarded the great iron gate came running. Streaming through the gate behind them came the whole mad mob of people. The Japanese had reached the railroad station.

Bullets screeched and crashed, and the people came running after the rolling trains. And then, and then . . . the passenger train unaccountably stopped. Now it was going back! It started rolling back—back to the station and the Japanese!

The soldier's hands cramped so tightly around the edge of Tien Pao's basket that the whole basket squeaked and groaned. "What is it? What is it?" Tien Pao yelled up at him.

"Don't you see?" the soldier yelled. "The last car came uncoupled in the station, and the fools are going back for it. . . . They can't! Oh, the fools! They can't!"

Still the passenger train kept backing. Now bullets clanged against the iron side of the locomotive, bullets smashed into the cars. Windows shattered. A man sagged through a window. People toppled off the roofs and out of open doorways. Still the train kept backing.

And for some bewildering reason, now the freight train stopped once more.

The soldier in the doorway shook his helpless fist, tears rolled unnoticed down his cheeks. "Now it's finished," he groaned. "The engineer got shot in the cab, I saw him fall. No one now is guiding that train, but it keeps backing. . . . It keeps backing."

With a groaning lurch the freight train got under motion. It chugged forward in a slow, agonizing crawl. It crept out of the station yard. It gathered speed. All along the track people were running hopelessly, uselessly, after it. A hail of bullets followed the train. And still the driverless passenger train kept slowly backing. Flames were shooting out of every station window now, but surely, slowly, the train backed into the burning station.

Tien Pao scrunched down in the deep basket to hide the sight. The soldier turned his head away.

CHAPTER SEVEN

THE HOUSE OF SIXTY FATHERS

There was no support in the open doorway of the rolling train. In the night the soldier, making room for himself, squatted down, squeezed the tall basket tightly between his knees, and placed both hands in a hard grip on the rim of the basket. In the basket Tien Pao had fallen asleep in a queer, uncomfortable, scrunched-up position. His legs straddled Glory-of-the-Republic, his hands were on the little pig's head—he was almost sitting on the little pig. Glory-of-the-Republic squirmed and wriggled.

In the deep dark of night before the dawn the train swayed and rocked as it leaned around the tight curve of a mountain. In the rocking doorway the basket teetered. The soldier's head nodded for a moment, his hands relaxed their hold on the rim of the basket.

The train leaned around the curve. The basket leaned, squeezed from between the sleeping soldier's knees, leaned out still farther—fell. Somehow as it fell it righted itself with the weight in its bottom. It fell flat on its bottom beside the speeding train. It bounced up, toppled over. It flung Tien Pao out beside the pounding wheels. Later the jumping basket spilled out Glory-of-the-Republic. It rolled away. Something under the train caught it, dragged it along.

In the doorway the soldier woke up with a start. The basket was not in the doorway! He leaped to his feet, he clutched the edge of the swaying doorway. There was a black mountain, and there was the night. The mountain echoed to the rolling of the train, but the mountain also beat back the sounds of a basket being shredded to pieces under the train. Not a muscle moved in the soldier's face as he stared down at the beating wheels. And then he shrugged and turned his head away.

The stunned Tien Pao crawled beside the train in the black darkness. He rolled himself away from the thundering wheels of the speeding train before he actually knew what had happened. Then he remembered the basket. The basket was gone!

The train had gone around the bend, even the sound of the train was gone, but Tien Pao still crawled beside the track, and as he crawled he placed his hand on the shredded bottom of the basket. He held the piece up to his eyes, stared at it uncomprehending, unbelieving.

A confused grunt came out of a deep ditch beside the track. Tien Pao flung the piece of basket from him and dived head-first into the black ditch. There at its narrow bottom lay Glory-of-the-Republic on his back, legs kicking the air. He was caught upside down in the narrow ditch, he couldn't struggle up—he grunted his distress and his disgust. Tien Pao grabbed him and held him. He hugged and squeezed the upside-down, kicking, grunting pig.

Suddenly Tien Pao pinched Glory-of-the-Republic's snout tightly shut. He heard voices. The night wasn't quiet any more. Sounds of voices came down the track. Dim, dark shapes came stumbling along over the railroad ties. Tien Pao slid down flat with the little pig in the dark ditch bottom.

More voices sounded. A mass of people came slowly around the bend. They struggled along under the weight of their belongings. These must be the poor who had evacuated Hengyang on foot when first the cannon had begun to thunder. They must have been walking for days to get this far. They trudged by. Women holding babies stooped by under the load of their household goods. Older children lugged younger children along. Some of the men were carrying an old father or mother piggy-back, and to the backs of the old ones high towering bundles had been strapped. They struggled by. The night became alive with their voices.

In a way it was good to lie at the bottom of the ditch listening to the many voices. To hear women and children talk out, their voices not hushed with fear. It meant that the Japanese had not yet reached this part of the country. . . . But that—that meant that now at last he, too, was free. Free! The sudden thought overwhelmed Tien Pao. He was free! He almost wanted to run to the people, yell it at them. He was alive and free, the Japanese had not got him!

He did not go. He stayed flat in the ditch, for among the voices he also heard children's voices in the dark—children whimpering to their mothers for food. He couldn't run to these hungry, homeless people; they would seize Glory-of-the-Republic—he was food. And even if little children wept from hunger in the night, Glory-of-the-Republic, too, had to be free. Alive and free!

But day was beginning to dawn. The first faint gray was beginning to streak the sky. And long before daylight really came, somebody in the endless stream of marching people would for no reason stumble to the edge of the ditch and discover him and Glory-of-the-Republic. Tien Pao looked up at the mountainous high rock looming up back of the ditch. These were his own people, but he couldn't stay in the ditch, nor follow the railroad track with them. For the sake of Glory-of-the-Republic he would once more have to take to the mountains.

When for the moment there were no voices above him on the track, Tien Pao crept noiselessly up the far side of the ditch. Hugging the deep shadows of the towering rock, he crept around the huge, sprawling, rock-strewn base until it was between him and the railroad track.

In the darkness Tien Pao peered up at the tall, somber rock. He poked about for a path. There did not seem to be a path. But he could not stay down below, and he did not dare wander farther from the railroad track. If he started to wander in this unknown country, he might blunder and circle back to the Japanese lines. The railroad track had to be his guide, it was the only thing to give him some sense of direction. He would have to follow it, the way he had followed the river. He'd hide on top of the rock, wait until this stream of people had passed, and then he'd set off down the track by himself—wherever it led him.

It struck Tien Pao that it might even be better

if there were no path up this sheer, steep rock. Hungry people did not climb useless, pathless rocks. But if he could somehow climb it, then he would be safe all day—he'd be looking down on the people, but they wouldn't be able to see him. Then a thought hit Tien Pao so hard it all but rocked him. It unnerved him. But it could be! It could just possibly be—his father and mother might easily be among these homeless wanderers on the track. Yes, it could be! He had reached this point in one night on the train, but these people on foot must have walked days and nights to get this far. These must be some of the first refugees from Hengyang. It could be! They could be among them!

If the guerrilla chief had been right when he said that a father would wait and a mother would not leave until the Japanese bayonets were at her back—why, then his father and mother would not even be among these first refugees. They would still be coming. And from the top of this high rock he could watch for them all day.

Almost frantic now to get to the top to watch the tracks for his father and mother, Tien Pao began the struggle up the almost sheer wall of rock. He dragged Glory-of-the-Republic up after him by the rope. He wouldn't give up and he wouldn't stop, no matter how much the little pig dragged and struggled against the impossible ascent. Tien Pao fought on, had to fight on, for other thoughts were crowding in among those first hopeful thoughts.

He couldn't let himself think these other thoughts: That his father and mother might have gone by some other road—there must be other roads out of Hengyang; that there was hardly a chance that they'd just happen to come down this particular track. He had to get up there and watch and watch. What else was there? If he did not find them, he was not alive and free—he was lost and homeless. Suppose tonight he did climb down and follow the railroad track, where would he go? Where in all China would he go? Where in all China was he to find his father and mother? And then what would become of him—lost, homeless, starving, lost! He had to climb, had to watch, and they had to come down the railroad track. There was no other hope.

At last Tien Pao pulled himself and Glory-of-the-Republic over the top of the towering crag. He was spent. Trembling with exhaustion and hunger, he stretched flat and peered down at the railroad track. It was strange. He could hear the constant mutter of their voices, but he could not seem to see the people down below. Dazed with weariness, sick with hunger, he lay staring down, but everything was spotty, everything danced. Big black ballooning spots floated between him and the people on the railroad track. They closed in, he could not see through them. It had taken so long to climb, the sun was already hot on his back. Tien Pao closed his eyes to clear them of the dancing and the lilting and the spots.

The warmth of the sun on the tall rock stole over Tien Pao, and he fell sound asleep. Glory-of-the-Republic rooted among the sparse grass and weeds, but then the tired pig cuddled down beside Tien Pao. In his sleep Tien Pao threw a protective arm over his little pig; together they slept their exhausted sleep. Down below, the voices in the endless procession of the homeless along the railroad track muttered on and on. Tien Pao slept on. Sunshine spilled over the great rock.

The evening sunshine lay warm against the face of the rock. Tien Pao awoke. In the evening hush a bugle had called. It called again. One bugle called from somewhere far away, but the fantastic rock on which Tien Pao lay took up the call and cast it back, and it was as if bugles sang everywhere.

But a bugle! Soldiers! The Japanese? But then Tien Pao let himself sink sweetly back as he remembered that he was in free country. These couldn't be Japanese, the bugle call must come from some Chinese barracks. Tien Pao wasn't fully awake yet; he stretched, rolled over on his back and looked at the sun. He struggled to arrange his sleepy thoughts —the sun was still rising, he hadn't slept too long. Now he must go and watch the railroad track for his father and mother and the baby sister.

Once more Tien Pao stretched himself, and yawned. He still felt warm and soft and confused. He looked at the sun again. But the sun was wrong! The morning sun had been behind the rock when he had climbed, but this sun shone from across the railroad track. He couldn't believe it. He reached out to shake the sleeping pig awake. Beyond the pig stood shoes! Two pairs of feet in heavy shoes!

In one scared jump Tien Pao grabbed Glory-of-the-Republic and was up and away on a stumbling run. In his confusion he would have run headlong over the edge of the cliff, but a hand reached out and grabbed him.

Tien Pao twisted in the man's grip. But he was white! Both men were white. They were soldiers—American soldiers. Tien Pao let himself droop and hang in the soldier's hold, he was limp with relief.

"Aw, you spoiled it," one of the Americans said to him. He tapped a small black box he held in his hand, and looked disgusted.

Tien Pao did not know what he had said. He did not know that the little black box was a camera, and that the soldiers had gone to the trouble of climbing the fantastic rock to take a picture. On top of the rock they had come upon a Chinese boy cuddled around a pig, both sound asleep. It had been too good to miss.

The soldiers made a lot of motions, grinned a lot, and at last Tien Pao understood that he was supposed to lie down again and snuggle up to Glory-of-the-Republic. He did what they wanted, but he nervously watched from under his eyelids for some explosion or red flash to come flaming out of the box the soldier was pointing at him. Nothing happened. The other soldier set Tien Pao back on his feet. It was all over, nothing had happened.

Tien Pao stood bewildered, but both soldiers now seemed very pleased. They patted Tien Pao's head, and one reached into his pocket and gave Tien Pao a wafer-thin slice of candy. The thin strip of candy was wrapped in green paper, with another wrapper of silver paper underneath the green. It puzzled Tien Pao—this surely must be extra-wonderful candy if the Americans had taken such pains to wrap so small a piece so thoroughly.

Tien Pao put the candy in his mouth. It lay sweet and thin on his tongue, but it did not begin to melt at all. He took it out again to look at it, turned it over—it stuck to all his fingers. Tien Pao stuck his fingers in his mouth to tear the candy off with his teeth. But the moment it was in his mouth it did not stick at all.

The two soldiers were laughing. They pointed to their teeth and made chewing motions. Tien Pao began to chew. He chewed and chewed, but the stuff simply would not chew away. At last Tien Pao just gulped and swallowed it. He rubbed his stomach to show the friendly soldiers how good it had been. They roared with laughter. Tien Pao did not laugh.

One of the soldiers looked at a watch bound to his wrist. He spoke quick words to the other soldier, and then they hastily strode away across the cliff and started to descend on the railroad side. Tien Pao was amazed—there *was* a path up the craggy rock, but in the dark he'd missed it. The two soldiers slithered and groped their way down the steep path on their hard shoes. Tien Pao looked down at Glory-of-the-Republic. The green wrapper of the queer candy lay at his feet; he stooped to pick it up. A lonely, starved, lost feeling welled up in Tien Pao. The hunger hit so fiercely—it must be that the strange candy in his stomach had awakened all his terrible hunger. It had put his stomach on fire. He was sick all over with hunger. Tien Pao dropped the green wrapper, picked up Glory-of-the-Republic, and silently started after the descending soldiers.

He was sick. Dizzy. Big ballooning blotches swept up before his eyes again. He had sense enough left to drop down on hands and knees on

the steep path to keep from falling headlong down the towering rock. He heard himself make a queer noise, then he blacked out.

When Tien Pao came to again, one of the soldiers was holding him in big, steady arms and carrying him down the steep path. It felt good to be held. Tien Pao just wanted to lie back, shut his eyes, but where was Glory-of-the-Republic? He must not be left behind. Tien Pao made sounds, he motioned, then he saw that the other man was coming on behind, carrying Glory-of-the-Republic. He closed his eyes. It was good to let go with the huge arms holding him. He'd slept all day, but he was so terribly sleepy.

When Tien Pao opened his eyes again, the men were taking him down a dirt road. There was a little open carriage standing at the side of the road. The soldier put Glory-of-the-Republic down, and sat down in the carriage behind a wheel.

A woman was walking down the little road. The soldier holding Tien Pao set him down, and pointed to the woman. "Ma-ma?" he asked. "You . . . want . . . to . . . go . . . home . . . to your . . . mother?" he said very slowly as if that would help Tien Pao understand.

Tien Pao half guessed what it might be the soldier was saying. He pointed far away from the walking woman, he made believe he was shooting, he tried to make the terrible sound a cannon makes, the swift rattle of rifle fire. He pointed to the woman, and spread his hands wide. He pointed to a man in a faraway rice paddy, and again he spread his hands. He waited anxiously.

The two soldiers talked to each other. Tien Pao listened to the strange, fast words. His lips moved along with them, so anxious was he to have the soldiers understand. If only they would take him along and give him food, then he could go back to the rock and watch for his father and mother. As if to help the soldiers understand, Tien Pao kept whispering it: "Please, understand. Oh, please, please, understand."

Suddenly the soldier picked him up and set him in the back seat of the carriage. He placed Glory-of-the-Republic in Tien Pao's lap. He stepped into the high seat himself and sat down next to Tien Pao. The man behind the strange wheel did things with his hands and feet. The carriage suddenly roared, shot ahead. It hopped and jumped and bounced in swiftness over the little road. It went still faster. The wind sang through Tien Pao's hair. The rushing wind revived him a bit, the sickness sank down from his eyes, but Tien Pao clung to Glory-of-the-Republic. Glory-of-the-Republic seemed to think he was running as fast as this wild, horseless carriage was rushing; he had his mouth wide open, he panted. But Tien Pao closed his eyes—in spite of the cooling wind, in spite of his hunger, he was sorry he had come. He wished the thing would stop.

Then it did stop. Tien Pao opened his eyes, but with a squeal and a shriek the mad carriage swung off the road into a narrow drive, and rushed up to a compound where stood a long wooden building. It stopped again and was so completely quiet, Tien Pao dared open his eyes and keep them open.

There were many soldiers about the compound. There were soldiers everywhere, and they all were white, but they didn't all have golden hair like the airman. They were all white, but their hair was of many different colors. The man behind the

wheel called to one of them. As he turned and came to the jeep, Tien Pao edged away from him. This man had green eyes—green eyes like a cat. And he had red hair! And he was hairy all over—hair even sprouted from his bare shoulders. He looked like a great ape to Tien Pao.

The hairy, green-eyed ape looked at Tien Pao, and then he yelled something that made all the other soldiers come running to look at Tien Pao and Glory-of-the-Republic. The loud, fast talk in the strange language flew, and everybody looked at him and seemed to talk about him. Tien Pao did not know where to cast his eyes.

All of a sudden the hairy one lifted Tien Pao out

of the jeep and carried him into the long house that must be the barracks of these soldiers. Tien Pao clung to Glory-of-the-Republic.

It was a strange house, this wooden house of the Americans. It was all one long room, and the room was all bedroom. It was full of windows, and full of beds—double beds, the one above the other. And even though it was still daylight, many men jumped out of the beds when Tien Pao with Glory-of-the-Republic was carried into the long room.

A half-naked soldier sat up in one of the beds and pointed to Glory-of-the-Republic and shouted something. Two soldiers ran up and tried to pull Glory-of-the-Republic out of Tien Pao's arms. Tien Pao wouldn't let go. They pointed to the door—they wanted Glory-of-the-Republic to stay outside. Tien Pao still wouldn't let go.

But the hairy man who had looked so horrible to Tien Pao grinned a big, understanding grin. He said something, and they let Glory-of-the-Republic be. Tien Pao loved him for that, even though he had green eyes and was red and hairy. He wished he could tell the good man what a proper pig Glory-of-the-Republic was, and that he knew how to live in houses.

Now the red-haired man set Tien Pao down and let out a loud shout. At that yell a Chinese came hurrying from somewhere, and all the men from outside came into the house, and all the men came down from their bunks. They crowded around Tien Pao and the Chinese man. The man said in Chinese: "I am an interpreter, knowing the strange language of these Americans. These men think you are lost."

"I am lost," Tien Pao said gravely. "Nor do I know where my father and mother are. I've just come from behind the Japanese lines, and from Hengyang."

When the interpreter translated that Tien Pao had just come from behind the Japanese lines, excited questions really rained down on him from all sides. The interpreter hastily told Tien Pao to tell his whole story from the beginning, and to tell it slowly. Tien Pao looked steadily at the interpreter and began to tell of the awful trip down the river. The interpreter took the words from Tien Pao's mouth and made them American, and all the men listened intently.

But when Tien Pao started to tell about the yellow-haired airman who had crashed, and whom the guerrillas had saved from the Japanese, all the men became so excited they forgot that Tien Pao couldn't understand them, and they began to question Tien Pao directly. Tien Pao could only wearily shake his head. But among all the questions there was one word the men kept saying again and again.

"What is this 'Hamsun' word that the men keep saying?" Tien Pao asked the interpreter.

"That is the name of the airman you saved," the interpreter told him.

"But do these men know him? Is he here, then? Is he one of them?"

"No, these sixty men belong to a bomb squadron. They fly the big bomber planes. Lieutenant Hamsun is flight leader of a fighter squadron. He flies a small fighter plane, and his fighter squadron is housed at the far end of this airfield, but he is now in the hospital at this field. However, all these men know him, and he told them of you."

"Is he well?" Tien Pao asked hastily.

"His wound is healing fast. . . . Oh, I've no doubt these men will take you to see him tomorrow—they seem to feel like fathers to you."

"They will?" Tien Pao said. "Oh, I'm glad." Oh, but this was exciting news. This was all so exciting. He wasn't even tired or hungry any more. "Oh, I'm glad," Tien Pao said all over again. He started laughing, and then he had a hard time stopping, even though the interpreter looked at him strangely. Oh, but this was exciting!

"But tell the men all you saw behind the Japanese lines. Tell them all—about Hengyang, too."

Tien Pao looked at the ring of faces—white faces, but friendly faces. They were all grinning at him.

All of a sudden Tien Pao felt so light and wonderful—so safe. Safe? Why, here he was safe. No one could hurt him here—not among sixty white airmen. Sixty, the interpreter had said. Sixty, all in one long wooden room with beds and windows. It was all so safe and strange and unbelievable.

Tien Pao began laughing again with the unbelievable wonder of it. He stopped himself. He mustn't laugh, these men wanted to know all. Tell them all—about Hengyang, too. Tell them about his village, and airplanes raining death and sampans sinking. And the three ducklings—the one in a riverful of water trying to scramble back into his dishpan home. The flaming plane and the airman tumbling out of it, and the Japanese shooting at him on top of the tall river cliff, and the long, scared, dark, hungry journey. Tell them all.

He was talking too fast—he could hear it, he was babbling. But not about those horrible things. No, not those horrible things! About the old toothless woman who had handed him a bowl of rice, and had made a guerrilla chief wait while he, Tien Pao, ate a second bowl of steaming rice.

But these men would not care about an old woman and a second bowl of rice. They couldn't even understand, except through the interpreter, but Tien Pao was in such a hurry to tell them all, he couldn't wait for the interpreter. He even tried to tell it with his eyes. He could feel his eyes getting bigger and bigger. And the white faces all around him—they were friendly faces, but they were getting dark, they were swimming away. Tien Pao started yelling at the faces swimming away. But he mustn't yell—these men were his friends, he mustn't yell at them. And he mustn't start crying now. There was that other old woman. She was mad, mad, mad! But she had brought him to the train, and she had hung half in the window, half out, and the train kept backing, kept backing. . . .

He had to yell! They must hear him. And he mustn't cry. He must smile—these were his friends. Tien Pao smiled, but the smile became a squeally laugh. What a silly, baby laugh. Why didn't he stop? The faces were becoming black, everything was black. Silly, silly . . .

Tien Pao slid to the floor.

Food odors stirred Tien Pao to life again. When he fluttered his eyelids open he found himself in one of the high bunks, all undressed, and with just a sheet thrown over him. Tien Pao dazedly looked at the red-haired soldier standing beside the bunk. But then his eyes went wide, he jerked himself to a sitting position—the man was holding a big tray, the tray was full of plates and bowls, all of them heaped high with hot, steamy, lovely food. Tien Pao's hand flew out to the tray. Suddenly the red-haired man stepped back—out of reach—the food was out of reach. Tien Pao felt himself going weak all over. He didn't try to reach the tray again, he just let himself fall back in the bed. He started crying. He retched. The fierce emptiness burning within him—the heavenly smell of hot food heaped on the tray—he couldn't help it, he had to cry. He cried and he hated. He did not understand, did not try to understand why the man had done that to him—he just hated.

The soldier stood there looking desperately at Tien Pao, and Tien Pao just wanted to cry and to hate him—hate him more and more. The big green-eyed, hairy ape!

The man began yelling, and he sounded fierce, and he must be yelling orders, for men went running out of the room—out of the doors at both ends.

At last one of them came back with the interpreter. The hairy ape stood there with the tray, talking long and earnestly to the interpreter over the heaped tray. The interpreter turned to the bed. "Master Sergeant Wilson, who is the chief of all these men, wants you to know that he fully intended to give you all the food. But when you awoke so suddenly, just that moment he'd begun to think that maybe it would do you much harm—all this food after so little. That is why he stepped back, but he has sent a man after the military doctor. The doctor will soon be here, and he will know."

"I understand," Tien Pao said wearily. He tried to look and smile at the hairy one who was the master sergeant of all these men, and who was called Sergeant Wilson, and who was a good man, but he couldn't help it, his eyes went only to the food on the tray. A last wrenching sob hiccuped out of him, but even so, it was almost sweet relief not to hate the good man so hard any more.

Sergeant Wilson saw Tien Pao's look. For a moment he stared around helplessly, but then he put the tray with food on the floor, and with his foot just shoved it toward the bed and out of Tien Pao's sight.

Glory-of-the-Republic must have been under the bunk, for now, grunting and snuffling, he barged right into the tray with dishes and bowls. Dishes rattled. Glory-of-the-Republic chewed and smacked. Tien Pao leaned over the edge of the high bunk and watched. In spite of himself, he began crying with greed and jealousy. Never had anything been too much for his little pig, but now he was jealous of the pig, and the hate came back. A big, murderous hate and rage stormed up in him—he could have killed Glory-of-the-Republic for eating, for smacking. He threw himself back hard on the bed so he couldn't see it, and stared stonily up at the ceiling.

The long room went very quiet. All of a sudden all the men seemed to have nothing to say to each other, and nothing to do but look at him! No, they sat on the edges of their bunks, watching the door, waiting for the doctor to come. The door opened, a new man came in. He must be an officer, for all the men jumped off their bunks and stood stiff and straight. At a word from the man, who must be the officer-doctor, they all came to gather around Tien Pao's bunk. They stood back, but the doctor stooped over Tien Pao, and Sergeant Wilson and the interpreter stepped up to stand beside him.

The doctor pulled the sheet back and Tien Pao lay naked before him and all the men. The doctor looked him all over, and peered down his throat and pulled back his eyelids, and grunted busy questions to the interpreter as he worked.

The interpreter asked: "The doctor wants to know, what have you been eating?"

Before Tien Pao could answer, a searing needle was run into his arm. Tien Pao winced, but even while he winced, the pain was already gone. There was an odd, thick feeling in his arm that seemed to steal all over him. Tien Pao kept a wary eye on the doctor while he told the interpreter: "I had four bowls of rice, but mostly I ate leaves. I didn't like grass."

The interpreter translated what Tien Pao had said. All the men made noises in their throats, but the doctor just grunted disgustedly and turned Tien Pao over. Then the doctor really made busy grunts, and he called all the men around and pointed to Tien Pao's bruises. He talked to the men. Somebody laughed a queer, short laugh.

"The doctor asked," the interpreter hastily explained to Tien Pao: "What did you do, jump off a few mountains?"

Tien Pao laughed. "I all but did that day when the Japanese shot down the plane of the Lieutenant Hamsun, for they shot at me, too, and I guess I tried to run faster than the bullets, and I fell and fell down that steep river cliff."

The interpreter did not translate, for the doctor was talking to the men, and while he talked he kept gently rubbing and rubbing Tien Pao's swollen stomach. The doctor sounded angry. Tien Pao hardly cared if the doctor was angry—it felt so good, his gentle rubbing.

At last the doctor pulled the sheet back over Tien Pao. He turned to Sergeant Wilson and he must be giving orders and instructions, for the chief sergeant nodded and nodded his head, and the interpreter nodded right along with him. Then the doctor gave Tien Pao a quick pat on the cheek, and turned and strode from the room. Immediately the whole room became busy. It almost seemed as if all the sixty airmen were suddenly rushing here, there, and everywhere doing busy things for him. It made Tien Pao feel warm and good. Surely the interpreter had been right when he'd said these men would be as sixty fathers to him—they acted just like fathers.

The doctor had hardly closed the door when the first man came trotting back from wherever he had gone, and now he handed a new tray to the chief sergeant, who had not moved from the side of the bed. On the tray lay one miserable thin slice of toasted bread. The man held one little glass of warm milk in his hand. He ordered Tien Pao through the interpreter to take tiny, slow sips, and Master Sergeant Wilson stood by and watched like a hawk to see that Tien Pao did just that. But Sergeant Wilson himself fed Tien Pao the slice of toast—a crumb at a time. He broke it into such tiny crumbs—he acted as if he were feeding a chicken, as if Tien Pao's arms were suddenly paralyzed and he couldn't feed himself. But it felt nice to be babied. It almost made Tien Pao a little moist around the eyes.

While the sergeant fed him crumb by crumb, two soldiers were standing by with a pail of warm water, and sponges. The moment Tien Pao finished the crumbs they began bathing him. But they dabbed and pecked with such clumsy gentleness at the old wounds and bruises, most of the water dripped onto the bed. Soaked as the bed got, the bath was soothing. It brought a wonderful, sleepy, cozy feeling to all of Tien Pao's tired, aching body. The men turned him over to bathe his back. Over the edge of the bunk Tien Pao could see the tip of Glory-of-the-Republic's snout. Glory-of-the-Republic was sound asleep. The little pig's chin rested in the tray among the empty dishes.

Tien Pao fell asleep looking at the sleeping Glory-of-the-Republic.

CHAPTER EIGHT

THE LONG DAY

Tien Pao sat up with a start. Where was he? Oh, yes, in the long house of the Americans with the many beds and windows. The sun was streaming through the windows. It was silent in the room. He was all alone. But where was Glory-of-the-Republic? Tien Pao lunged to the edge of the high bunk. There was nothing under the bunk. There wasn't a sound anywhere in the room. Where was Glory-of-the-Republic? Maybe the Americans had butchered him!

Naked as he was, Tien Pao tumbled from the high bunk and tore through the empty room and out the door, calling and calling Glory-of-the-Republic. Oh, there was Glory-of-the-Republic in the yard! Tien Pao went limp with relief. There he was in a tipped-over barrel in the compound—roped to the barrel.

Tien Pao flew to his little pig, and since Glory-of-the-Republic couldn't get out because of the rope, the naked Tien Pao crawled into the barrel with him to hug and pet and comfort him. The enormous relief made him silly. They hadn't butchered Glory-of-the-Republic—he might have known—they'd given him a very proper barrel-house with straw in it!

Suddenly the interpreter stood before the barrel. He was indignant. "Now, you are not to run outdoors naked! Your sixty fathers would be horrified. In America people do not run out of doors naked, not even boys—I suppose because they have plenty of clothes."

Tien Pao sat up in the barrel. "Oh, yes—my sixty fathers. They are like fathers to me, aren't they?"

"Ah, but you don't know the full extent of it yet! The men of the Sixteenth Bombardment Squadron—that is what your sixty fathers are called—last night adopted you because you helped save the Lieutenant Hamsun, and have no father and mother, and are lost and starved."

Tien Pao looked at the man in stunned bewilderment. "Sixty fathers? And I'll live in the long house with them? But I have a father and a mother!"

"The house is called a barracks," the interpreter evaded.

"I don't want sixty fathers," Tien Pao exploded. "I have a father and mother. . . . Oh, I'm not ungrateful," he added hastily. "But don't you understand? I have a father and mother, and I must find them and the baby sister. I have to find them!"

"Yes, yes," the interpreter said uncomfortably. "But where? You must face it, Tien Pao. Where in all China? When there are thousands upon thousands of lost war children like you, I can tell you you were extraordinarily lucky to be picked up by the Americans, and now to be adopted by them. . . . Of course, this isn't permanent—only until such time as your father and mother are found," he added weakly. "The men will do all they can to help you find them, but until then you will live with them. And I can tell you," he coaxed, "you'll live like a prince. You should be thankful."

"I am thankful," Tien Pao whispered, but his lips trembled. He stared out before him. "And yesterday when I could have watched for them coming down the railroad, I fell asleep," he said aloud to himself. "And when I awoke I thought only of my hunger and went with the two Americans."

The interpreter shrugged helplessly. "You must

face it—it is most unlikely. It would be the smallest chance. The railroad is but one road out of Hengyang, there are other roads, and so many homeless people—hordes of them. You shouldn't feel guilty and reproach yourself."

"I knew there were other roads," Tien Pao said somberly, "but I also knew if I watched from the rock they would come around the bend of the railroad track. First my father, and a few steps behind him my mother, carrying the baby sister. I knew that, but I slept."

"Tien Pao, you are accusing yourself for nothing! All that was little more than a hopeless hope. And I—I'm a poor comforter, but I don't know what to say. Anyway, you shouldn't be in the barrel, and you must get back to bed. The doctor ordered it."

Tien Pao stubbornly shook his head. "No, I'm going back to the rock. There still must be people coming—those yesterday must have been the first ones. And the guerrilla chief told me that my father and mother would wait for me in Hengyang until the last, so they would be among the last, and then they'd still be coming. And I believe that, because I have to believe it!" He grabbed Glory-of-the-Republic's rope in nervous haste. "Don't you see that I must get back to watch for them?" he urged. "Where are all—all the fathers?" He was behaving badly, ungratefully. Somehow he couldn't help himself,

something inside him seemed to be driving him, making him say things, pulling him back to the rock to watch.

"The men are at work at the airfield, or they're on a bombing run—anyway, they won't be back until evening." The interpreter half turned at the sound of a jeep as if hoping it might be some of the Americans to help him out of his difficult situation. It was the doctor! He came striding across the compound straight to the barrel.

The interpreter stood before the officer-doctor in an apologetic half-bow, evidently explaining and explaining why Tien Pao stood naked in the yard instead of being in bed. Tien Pao watched the doctor anxiously. Now the doctor would order him back to bed. He'd run away—back to the rock—he'd slip out of bed the moment the doctor was gone and the interpreter was busy. But where were his clothes?

"Where are my clothes? What did you do with them?" Something inside of him seemed to be urging him to yell it at the interpreter. But the doctor was talking so earnestly, and while waiting for the doctor to finish, Tien Pao evolved a shrewder plan. He wouldn't ask for his clothes, it would make them suspicious. He'd go willingly to bed, but the moment they were out of the room he'd hunt for his clothes, and if he couldn't find them, he'd wrap himself in one of the blankets that lay folded at the foot of every bunk, free Glory-of-the-Republic, and sneak out to the rock. Tien Pao began surreptitiously undoing the knot in Glory-of-the-Republic's rope.

The interpreter turned to him. "Now, listen to this. I was all wrong. This doctor thinks it would be good for you to go to the rock to watch for your parents. . . . Now, I do not know whether I'm to tell you all this—these Americans are babying you so—but you'll have to face it sooner or later, and you've faced so much, I think you can handle this, too. . . .

"Well, then, this doctor thinks you are acting the way you are because as yet you can't face up to the fact that you have come to the end of the road. All these days and nights you believed you were going back to your father and mother, but now there remains but the small, forlorn hope that you may still find them by watching from the rock. But as I said before—where in all China among the thousands? Of course, it is true, there is a chance they might come down that railroad track, and while there's just a little hope . . ." The interpreter fell silent as he poked around in his mind, trying to find right words. "I don't know whether I say the right things," he said unhappily.

"In the middle of the night I woke up and lay thinking long," Tien Pao told the man gravely, "and I thought all those same thoughts. They were hard thoughts to think, but I thought them through, and that is why I must go to the rock to watch for my parents until the last refugee from Hengyang has passed."

The interpreter drew a big, relieved breath. "Then if you understand it—the doctor says he will take you out to the rock in his jeep. I'm to get your clothes and fix a small lunch so that you can stay there all day."

The interpreter hurried away. Tien Pao walked up to the doctor and quietly laid his cheek against the man's hand—it had to express all his gratitude. Then he busied himself with the knot in Glory-of-the-Republic's rope.

"Now, look at this!" The interpreter was back. "Last night while you slept, your sixty new fathers had me trot to the village that lies beyond the airfield to buy shoes and underwear for you. And look at this! They had me sit up most of the night, cutting down one of their uniforms to your size. They want you to be in American uniform, exactly like theirs."

Tien Pao stared at it. "It is too much. It is too much," he stammered brokenly. "And I have been an ungrateful wretch. It is too much." But he was dithering with impatience to get into the bright, clean uniform. And when he was dressed, he looked proudly down at himself and twisted his head every which way to see every part of the smart, sharply pressed uniform. The doctor stepped back several paces to admire him properly. He threw Tien Pao a smart salute. Tien Pao laughed excitedly, but his face immediately straightened again. He looked anxiously at the doctor. "I am an ungrateful wretch," he mumbled shamefacedly, "but how soon can we go to the rock?"

"You are not a wretch," the interpreter said, stepping back, proud of his own handiwork. "We understand. The doctor understands."

"The sun is shining," Tien Pao told the doctor in Chinese to explain his dreadful, driving hurry. "A whole long day I can watch, and watch without any hunger, and I have slept a whole long night." He took the doctor's hand and gripped it, but it was to hurry the man to the jeep.

The interpreter got into the back seat of the jeep. He had a paper carton with Tien Pao's lunch in it, and a huge paper bag with potato peelings for Glory-of-the-Republic. Tien Pao laughed delightedly and stroked the creased trousers of his new uniform. "Everybody here is wonderful even to my pig."

"If that were all," the interpreter said. "But the doctor has planned a great surprise for you late this afternoon when he comes back with the jeep to take you from the rock to the barracks—he does not want you to walk the distance. By that time your sixty fa—the men should be back at the barracks, too."

"They are my sixty fathers," Tien Pao said gravely. "I was very bad there in the barrel. Sixty fathers and a house, and my pig has a barrel with straw." He laughed exultantly, but he turned from the interpreter and the laugh erased itself. He knew only too well why the doctor had planned the surprise—the doctor did not expect him to have found his father and mother when he came back with the jeep to take him from the rock.

In English the interpreter repeated what Tien Pao had said, and the doctor nodded and smiled, but Tien Pao was relieved when at that moment he saw the rock. He pointed to it excitedly. There was his rock, and there lay the railroad track, and, marvelously, people were still coming down the track! Oh, not many at this moment, but they still straggled along. And there now came a whole party of ten around the bend!

The doctor stopped the jeep and Tien Pao got out with Glory-of-the-Republic and his bag and carton. He hesitated. "Would the good doctor wait until I am on top of the rock? These people are hungry, and my pig is food."

"Oh, we'll wait," the interpreter promised without even asking the doctor, and the doctor nodded his head—he understood. "We'll wait," he said with a grin, imitating the interpreter.

Tien Pao had lain on the rock for hours. The sun had gone over and was shining in his face now. The afternoon was passing, the sun shone bright and clear on the tracks below. Tien Pao lay concealed between a couple of huge boulders. An old woman passed along on the track. He could almost count the deep wrinkles in her old face. But she was not a woman who had come far, she merely came down the track with a basket of grass that she had cut. She was full of wrinkles. Tien Pao looked into the afternoon sun—there was nothing to watch on the track.

He was hungry. The lunch had been eaten long hours ago. It had not taken long—one thin slice of bread, a little jar with milk, and a small banana. The sweet taste of lovely banana still lay along Tien Pao's tongue. He tasted it again by poking the tip of his tongue between his teeth. Glory-of-the-Republic had finished the bag of peelings hours ago, had eaten the bag, and now he was eating Tien Pao's carton.

Tien Pao wiped his eyes, which were blurred from his sun-staring. He could hide it from himself no longer. The endless procession of homeless stragglers from Hengyang had stopped! Oh, now and then a little family group still came jogging around the bend, but mostly those who passed were old people, slow old people who walked a little, rested a little. They'd just suddenly sit down on one of the rails, sit and stare without raising their heads.

Tien Pao thought he heard voices. He waited, but nothing came around the bend of the railroad track. Tien Pao anxiously stared at the sun again. Again he thought he heard voices. At last an old man came around the bend, all by himself. He was talking loudly to himself. In the clear sunlight Tien Pao could see the old stumps of teeth as he talked.

Below the rock the old man abruptly sat down, he searched himself as if for food. He moaned a little. On top of the rock Tien Pao felt miserable with him, feeling just what the old man felt. If he hadn't eaten everything, he could at least have thrown the banana down in the carton, but Glory-of-the-Republic had eaten even the carton.

The old man was pushing himself up again to stagger on. Glory-of-the-Republic wasn't in any danger from him—the old man couldn't possibly climb the rock. Tien Pao stood up. "Grandfather," he called down, "are you from Hengyang?"

"Eh?" The old man was startled. "You frightened me, lad," he said when he had at last located Tien Pao. "Yes, I am from Hengyang. Why?"

"Are there more coming, more families? Are there a lot more people who possibly waited until the last, and did not leave until after the Japanese had taken most of the town?" Tien Pao held his breath.

"It seemed to me I was the last one," the old man said slowly. "It seemed to me I was so slow, they all passed who were once behind."

"Did—did a small family pass you? A tall man with big strides, a young mother, carrying a little female child?"

The old man spread his hands wearily. "My son, those are foolish questions. There were so many."

"Yes," Tien Pao said in a small voice.

The old man started on, but then he turned again. "Grandson, have you anything to eat up there? I—well, I hunger."

Tien Pao mournfully shook his head. The old man pressed his lips together and moved on.

After the brief talk the silence on the rock and along the whole railroad track seemed to close in completely. A choking feeling lumped in Tien Pao's throat. It was no use fooling himself any longer, and he had known it all along—it was hopeless.

He'd known it all along—they wouldn't come. They had either passed by, or had gone along some other road to almost anywhere. Still Tien Pao stayed on the rock. He could not seem to get himself to go back to the barracks of the white soldiers

—the going down the rock, the going back to the sixty men would somehow prove that his mother and father were gone, and that all hope was gone.

Tien Pao tried not to think, tried not to look down the empty railroad track. He made himself admire his uniform once more. He made himself very busy brushing the dust from it. He stroked the creased trousers back into a press, patted them smooth. He felt a lump—there was still another pocket he had not found before. So many pockets in these strange clothes! Tien Pao poked in the pocket. His mouth fell open as he withdrew a wad of Chinese yen notes. A roll of money! Not only had they given him a new uniform, they had stuffed it with yen. Truly these amazing Americans did not know the value of yen! Tien Pao started to count. Suddenly he ran to the outer edge of the rock. "Grandfather, Grandfather," he called out as loud as he could. He knew real, deep, hopeless hunger, and what it did. He'd give the old man much yen for food—for a big meal, and then for meals tomorrow and the next day. "Grandfather, Grandfather!"

The old man had passed out of hearing. The huge rocks along the railroad track mocked back: "Grandfather, Grandfa—aa—" Tien Pao looked at the sun. Should he run after the old man, or wait until sunset. There was no one on the rock anyway. . . . He turned for a last look, and then his heart stopped cold. Around the bend came a tall man striding, behind him a stooped woman came. A baby was on her back! Tien Pao trembled. His skin went cold. With shaky hands he rubbed his blurred, smarting eyes. He kept his fists there—in his eyes; he did not dare to make sure. Wait a tiny moment —catch his breath. He couldn't breathe!

His heart pounding, Tien Pao dropped his fists a little, tried to stare over them, tried to find just the baby—he'd know by the baby. But if he looked first at the woman, and if it was his mother, he'd plunge straight down the rock to get to her. He knew he would!

He saw the man first. It wasn't his father. It was another family. Tien Pao turned his back so he would not have to see the woman with the baby pass. He stood wooden and completely empty, waiting for the sound of their scuffling feet to fade. After this little family was gone he'd go back to the house of the sixty fathers—the barracks. He could not go through this again.

Suddenly the man was yelling up at him. "Boy, up there, did I hear you calling your grandfather? Did you lose your grandfather?"

Tien Pao could not answer, could not turn at once. The whole little family must be waiting, he heard no scuffling of feet.

At last Tien Pao turned. Just the man was waiting. The woman had kept walking, and for that Tien Pao was thankful. "Are you from Hengyang?" he managed to ask the man.

"No, we are from a village many li this side of Hengyang. The Japanese are now holding all of Hengyang, and are beginning to move again. They're coming on."

"Beyond Hengyang?" Tien Pao said, stunned. "Did you—did you anywhere pass a little family just like yours from Hengyang? Just like yours?"

The man looked up. "Your family?"

Tien Pao nodded.

"I'm sorry, son—nothing like that. All we passed from Hengyang were a few old and sick and dying—the stragglers. But you were calling out for your grandfather. Did you lose your grandfather, too?"

Tien Pao dumbly shook his head. He could talk no more. The man still stared up, and Tien Pao knew he was curious about the uniform but too polite to ask. He said nothing, and the man moved on to catch up with his wife. He took long strides.

Now Tien Pao could not stay on the rock. It was too awful staring at the silent, empty railroad track. It was over. It was done. The Japanese had the whole country around Hengyang. Nobody was coming from Hengyang any more. Tien Pao grabbed up Glory-of-the-Republic and slithered and plunged down the steep path. He ran down the little dirt road, but suddenly he turned and charged back to the railroad track and ran hard along the track. The young family was gone, but the old man still groped along. Tien Pao caught up with him. He stuffed yen into the hand of the astonished old man. "For your hunger, Grandfather," he panted. "To buy much food."

"It will go well with you, son. It will certainly go well with you!" the old man said fervently.

Tien Pao turned and ran back along the railroad track to the little dirt road below the rock.

CHAPTER NINE

BREAK DOWN THE MOUNTAINS

Tien Pao hesitated long at the door of the barracks. The sixty fathers were back. He could hear shuffling of feet inside, someone coughed, but otherwise they were unusually silent—these noisy, loud-talking Americans. It seemed strange to stand at the door of a barracks and that the barracks was his house. Was he supposed to knock, or just walk in? In time Tien Pao remembered Glory-of-the-Republic—the little pig had to go into the barrel, he could not be in the house. If only they knew, if only he could make them understand, that a pig could be proper, and that Glory-of-the-Republic was a very proper pig.

Tien Pao started to tie Glory-of-the-Republic to the barrel. Across the yard he eyed the closed door; it would make it all the harder to go in without his pig. Glory-of-the-Republic set up a struggle, he did not want to be left behind in the barrel. Tien Pao picked him up again and with the pig in his arms went back to the door. It seemed somehow wrong that the door of these foreign men was his door, too. It really was, they really had adopted him, but as he stared at the closed door, Tien Pao felt so sad and forlorn that it made his throat ache and his eyes feel tight and tired.

He whispered to his pig, trying to get up courage to push the door open. He wished someone would come, so he could go in with him. He turned hopefully at the distant sound of a motor, wanting it to be a jeep with some of the men—that would make it much easier. But the distant motor sound was a fighter plane. It glinted silver in the late afternoon sun as it slid out of the sky down to the far end of the distant airfield. It was exactly like the plane the Lieutenant Hamsun had gone down in.

Then under the motor sounds was another sound, nearer, and this was a jeep! It turned from the

road into the drive and raced toward the compound. It was the doctor! Oh, he'd forgotten! And now the doctor had driven out to the rock all for nothing. Tien Pao almost shoved the door open to plunge into the room, but he had Glory-of-the-Republic with him. Tien Pao felt cornered. He turned to face the doctor.

The doctor was not alone in the jeep. But the sun's reflection on the windshield made it difficult to see who was with him. It wasn't the interpreter. Could it . . . was it? It was! It was his yellow-haired airman, his river god. The doctor had brought the airman from the hospital to see him. That was the surprise! With a yell Tien Pao flew to the jeep, he all but dropped Glory-of-the-Republic. "Lieutenant Hamsun! Lieutenant Hamsun!" He was proud that he could shout out the name.

The doctor had got out of the jeep, but Lieutenant Hamsun was slow, his leg must still be stiff. Tien Pao could not wait. He leaped into the jeep, slid over the seat, and laid his head against the man's chest. "Lieutenant Hamsun." Oh, they had no words, but now they'd be able to talk through the interpreter, tell each other all the things they'd wanted to tell each other that long day in the cave, that night in the mountains, and all the things that had happened since. Tien Pao was so excited he couldn't hold still, he pulled away, proudly showed the airman his uniform. He laughed excitedly and even pulled out the wad of yen to show to the lieutenant.

Lieutenant Hamsun said something, but it was suddenly completely lost in the crashing roar of a fighter plane that had seemed to come from nowhere and was skimming tightly over the roof of the barracks. It flashed like silver fire along the roof and was gone in its own roar. Even so, in that flash of a moment the pilot of the plane must have seen and recognized Lieutenant Hamsun in the jeep, for the plane had waggled its wings and Lieutenant Hamsun had waved at the pilot.

Tien Pao stared after the plane with amazed mouth wide open. The interpreter and some of the sixty men came running out of the house, but Glory-of-the-Republic had scuttled under the jeep.

"It is called buzzing the barracks," the interpreter called out to Tien Pao in Chinese, proud of his knowledge of such things.

Tien Pao hardly heard him. He stared toward where the plane had disappeared almost in the wink of an eye—that quick, that fast. And now there stirred in Tien Pao a great new idea.

He laid an urgent hand on Lieutenant Hamsun's arm. Totally forgetting that the man couldn't understand him, he talked earnestly, rapidly, his words tumbling over each other because of the great hope and the great thought that had come to him out of the roaring swiftness of the silver plane that had scraped over the house and had been gone before its sound was gone. Lieutenant Hamsun listened as intensely as Tien Pao talked. Without taking his eyes from Tien Pao's face, he motioned to the interpreter to come close. "It is this." Tien Pao began all over again without interrupting the flood of his words. "It is the hope the swift plane gave me, and if it should fail, then I will gladly be the adopted son of these sixty men, for they are like fathers to me, and the good doctor, too. . . . But if the train was swift, the plane is a hundred times faster. And as I watched from the rock, the last stragglers passed from Hengyang, and now there will be no more, for I was told that the Japanese have all of Hengyang and are coming on.

"But those who passed in the night and those who passed that whole day while I lay sleeping on the rock are still walking somewhere, and a plane in all its swiftness could overtake them in moments.

"Oh, I am asking much, I know. . . . But it's my father and my mother, and my little sister. Could then the Lieutenant Hamsun take me in a plane down the railroad track until we come to such a point that the refugees have not yet reached? Then I would know. Isn't there still enough daylight left, even after the sun sets, that if my father and mother were not on the railroad track—would it—couldn't the plane still follow the other roads from Hengyang?"

Tien Pao was out of breath and aghast at his own desperate boldness to make such an enormous request. All the men were standing around. . . . "It is not that I'm ungrateful," he mumbled, although the interpreter was busy translating what he had said. Then, overcome by the enormity of what he had done, he stared stony-faced at the floor of the jeep while the interpreter's strange words that were *his* words went on and on.

Then words flew between Lieutenant Hamsun and the doctor standing beside the jeep. Tien Pao did not dare look up. Oh, he wasn't ungrateful! He was almost bursting with gratitude, and with happiness at seeing Lieutenant Hamsun again, but the plane had come over, and the thoughts had come, and the hope. . . .

The interpreter must have seen Tien Pao's face turn colors as the two men argued, for he said in a low voice: "The Lieutenant Hamsun wants to do just what you said—right now. But the doctor won't let him because of his hurt leg, even though the doctor agrees that it ought to be done. He wants someone else to do it, but the lieutenant won't hear of it. He insists he is the one to do it, since you so greatly helped him." The interpreter chuckled. "Now he's telling the doctor he'll stay in his old hospital an extra month if he'll just let him do this one thing."

"And my—my sixty fathers?" Tien Pao whispered urgently.

"Oh, you haven't lost face with them either," the interpreter assured him. "They are all for it, because they are all for you, but just doubtful that the Lieutenant Hamsun should do it. Don't be ashamed

—they understand. Master Sergeant Wilson just said it to you. He said: 'You're all right, Tien Pao.' And that means much in the language of the Americans."

Tien Pao quickly glanced at the sergeant, and Sergeant Wilson winked at him and nodded. At that moment the doctor suddenly shoved Tien Pao over, and got behind the wheel of the jeep. The jeep roared, and Glory-of-the-Republic shot from under it. But Sergeant Wilson caught the little pig neatly between his legs and handed him to the interpreter, who got into the back seat of the jeep, and there he sat with the pig in his lap. Tien Pao sat between Lieutenant Hamsun and the doctor, and he could have wept, so great was his relief. To prevent it he started babbling to Lieutenant Hamsun, telling him all the things he had wanted to say from the first time they had met. The interpreter leaned over Glory-of-the-Republic and listened and translated. They had so much to tell each other that without Tien Pao's noticing it they arrived at the airfield.

The jeep stopped, and there stood a small plane near a building. Lieutenant Hamsun climbed carefully down from the jeep, and limped to the building. That was to get clearance and permission to take the plane up, the interpreter knowingly explained to Tien Pao. The doctor had also gone into the building, but now he came back with a sandwich and milk for Tien Pao, and a whole dozen bananas for Glory-of-the-Republic. He grunted at the little pig and teased him with a banana, but then with a quick smile for Tien Pao he walked away. Lieutenant Hamsun emerged from the building, and motioned Tien Pao and the interpreter to the plane. When he noticed the doctor was gone, he almost ran to the plane with Tien Pao.

There was enough room for all of them on the small plane. "This is not a fighter, this is a Beechcraft," the interpreter explained. "But you'll be able to see better and it is swift enough so that we can easily cover the railroad track and and also the two dirt roads leading from Hengyang long before darkness falls."

Lieutenant Hamsun was busy in the pilot's seat. Glory-of-the-Republic was busy eating the last peel of the last banana, but when the plane's motor suddenly roared, the little pig scuttled between Tien Pao's feet and flattened himself so tightly against the floor, Tien Pao almost had to pry him loose. He hoisted the little pig to his lap. By that time the plane was already running like a possessed thing across the flat field. Tien Pao held Glory-of-the-Republic up to the window. The little pig got a wild look in his eyes, and shrank back when he saw the speed at which a building, standing trucks, and a mountainside rushed by. He had clenched his teeth down on the banana peel in his first scare. It still hung limp from his mouth, and his scared ears flapped as limply as the banana peel.

Tien Pao's own throat felt too narrow and too full as suddenly the plane bounced up, took another higher bounce, and was a thing of earth no more. Now just a rooftop was beside them for a second, the next second the tip of a mountain, but already it fell away, and then there were clouds. Earth had dropped away, now the clouds too fell away as the plane broke through them. Tien Pao clenched his teeth and closed his eyes, for a sickness rose, and his stomach seemed to rush up faster than the plane rushed up from the earth.

The interpreter poked Tien Pao, shoved a stick of gum at his clenched mouth, and motioned him to chew hard. Tien Pao dared hardly unclench his teeth for fear his stomach would pop out. He closed his eyes again.

Again the interpreter poked him. Lieutenant Hamsun wanted them to come forward. To Tien Pao's amazement, he could walk over the floor as if the plane were a level, flat, standing thing and not something hurtling through air. Lieutenant Hamsun motioned Tien Pao to the seat beside him. The interpreter stood behind them, leaning over

Tien Pao's shoulder, looking and looking. Now Lieutenant Hamsun pointed down.

Tien Pao gasped in surprise. The airfield was gone. Below them was a village—why, this must be the village where the interpreter had gone to buy him shoes and underwear. They were flying low over the village, following the crooked market street. The street was full of people—it must be market day in the village. Down below, a rickshaw boy was shouting and clearing a path for himself and his rickshaw down the packed street. Tien Pao could see him yelling.

A crowd had gathered at the corner of the market street and an alley. They stood around a dentist, who had a man in a chair and was pulling his teeth. The man sat head tilted back, his agonized eyes stared into the sky. Tien Pao looked down into his wide-open mouth. For a moment it was as if he and Tien Pao were staring into each other's eyes. Tien Pao gave no thought to the man, but hugged himself in utter relief. Oh, it would be easy! If he could look into a mouth, even though it was just for a flash, he could surely recognize his father and mother, for that would not even take a flash. He hugged himself again. You saw so clearly, even though it was just for a moment. It would need only a moment, an instant.

Already the village was long gone, and now below them stretched two narrow steel bands, glinting in the rays of the evening sun. The railroad track! But it stretched empty, straight, and deserted before them.

"Lieutenant Hamsun will first fly along the railroad toward Hengyang as far as it is safe to go," the interpreter explained beside Tien Pao's ear. "Then he'll turn and fly in the other direction until there is not a single refugee anywhere along the track."

Tien Pao nodded and leaned forward over the pig in his lap. Glory-of-the-Republic began finishing the banana peel he found clenched between his teeth. The little pig was already used to flying. Tien Pao laughed. He was laughing! The sickness was gone with the laugh. His stomach had slid back to where it had always been and where it belonged. Oh, flying was wonderful and effortless and easy and swift!

Down below, the railroad track lay absolutely empty, and now the plane rose higher, still higher. Then far below them, far in the misty distance, rose a town, row on row of roofs. A silver ribbon coiled crookedly through the town among the straight rows of buildings. But where the river crawled the blackened buildings had no roofs, yawned empty at the sky. Tien Pao gave a start of recognition. "Hengyang?"

Lieutenant Hamsun nodded.

The plane was banking, turning, and now it flew away from Hengyang. Flew back along the empty railroad track. Again that start of recognition jerked Tien Pao upright—why, there already was the rock on which he had watched. They were back! It was unbelievable, the speed of an airplane—here they were back and even on a train it had taken a whole night, and on foot—oh, his father and mother could have walked days and nights on end, but the airplane in moments would overtake all their walking.

Tien Pao leaned hard over his pig, sat rigid, eyes riveted on the two steely ribbons of track. He mustn't miss them—it needed but a moment, but he mustn't look away even for a moment, he mustn't miss a single person down there on the track.

Now the plane started down from its height and the track rose and neared. Here people plodded down below, and the plane levelled off and swept over them. Here again were the strung-out stragglers. Again the start of recognition came over Tien Pao. There was the little family—the last ones—the man he had talked to walking on ahead with long strides. He looked up at the plane. But the old toothless man was nowhere—he must be eating and resting in some village.

But the low airplane snarling and sweeping down at them threw the people on the tracks into panic. Some looked up in terror, some just ducked their heads and plodded on, but others threw themselves flat, face down; some even bolted to the roadside ditch and threw themselves into it. And Tien Pao understood, for these people knew only that planes rained death, the only way that he had known planes until these last two days.

"Could we please fly higher?" he urged the interpreter. "I am sure that I will know my father and mother in the flash of a second from almost any height."

Lieutenant Hamsun understood, for already he was flying high enough so that the people down below hardly looked up. They just trudged on under their loads. The plane flew on. Sometimes the coiled-spring start of recognition jerked Tien Pao forward as some little family group appeared below them. Each time the two men would turn their heads and look at him. But each time Tien Pao had to shake his head. He wanted it too much—too hard—he must stop fooling himself. . . .

They weren't there! They weren't among the endless stream of refugees along the railroad track. The plane had passed them all. It still swept on, but now the railroad lay empty. Still Lieutenant Hamsun raced on. Tien Pao laid his hand on his arm, and shook his head. "They are not on the track."

Lieutenant Hamsun knew without the interpreter needing to translate. He spoke to the interpreter instead.

"The Lieutenant Hamsun wants to know—do you want to go back along the railroad track? Then we'll be facing the people below."

Tien Pao shook his head. "They are not on the track. I know, for I would have known them in a moment. I would rather go by way of the other roads."

Now the plane had swept along both the narrow dirt roads. It had followed each one all the way until there were no refugees in either direction. All the distance in between Tien Pao had looked down at refugees by the thousands, strung out along both roads miles upon miles, but his father and mother had not been among them. The sun was going down. On the last road there was now only a farmer leading his water buffalo home from the day of plowing. He was carrying a little girl on his shoulder. The little girl looked up at the plane and waved. Tien Pao turned his head away. "Would the lieutenant on our way back to the airfield and the house of sixty fathers follow the railroad track once more?" he asked heavily.

The plane at once set out cross-country. Tien Pao sat staring straight ahead. He did not care about the country below, or care about anything; he knew only too well that his last hopeless request to go back along the railroad track was just that—hopeless. He'd known surely that first time that his father and mother were not among the refugees on the railroad track. It just prolonged the last little hope and tiny possible doubt a little longer, until the time would come when he'd once more have to say: "They are not there." Then the plane would let down on the airfield, then they'd ride in the jeep to the house of the sixty fathers, and then there'd be no more hope. There'd just be emptiness and the final hard fact, which was that he was lucky, among all these thousands upon thousands of the homeless, to be adopted by his sixty American fathers. He somehow had to get used to that fact, but now he only felt empty.

"May I go to sit alone back there in the plane?" he whispered. It was doubtful that the men had heard the whisper, but both men nodded together, and the interpreter took Glory-of-the-Republic, and Tien Pao slid from the seat. Behind the men's backs Tien Pao pulled himself along, but he did not sit in the seat, he sat on the floor, put his arms on the seat, put his head in his arms, and held himself very still. It was not necessary to see any more what was down below—they were not there.

Much later the interpreter called out to him:

"Tien Pao, this you must see. I think the Lieutenant Hamsun really wants you to see this, for he has taken us far around to where they are building a great new airfield beside the railroad track. It is much farther down the railroad track than we went the first time, far beyond the refugees. . . ."

Tien Pao got up—he knew they were doing it to distract him—and he dutifully walked back to the glassed-in nose of the plane and looked down. He gasped. Straight below them lay a huge airfield. It was enormous. It stretched flatly away, and many little roads ribboned away from it, winding in and out among endless buildings. From here high in the sky it was as if a giant hand had just dropped clusters of buildings in clumps, had strewn other lone buildings helter-skelter, and then had wound the ribbon roads between them. Trucks and jeeps scuttled like water bugs along the little threads of lines that were the roads. Down over the flat stretches of grassy field crawled the flat beetles that must be huge bombing planes.

Their own plane, still circling the field, dropped lower, things got bigger. Down slid the plane. It made an enormous circle of the field at the new level. Now the mountains all around the field began rising up next to the plane. The plane banked. Tien Pao held his breath. For a moment it had almost looked as if one wing was going to scrape the side of a mountain.

The last rays of the evening sun lay against the mountainside. Tien Pao could see the shadow of their plane sliding along the mountain. It slid over men working on the mountainside. They did not even look up as the shadow slid over them, they kept swinging big hammers. Some leaped from one pile of rocks to another pile, nimbly—like the little black goats of the mountains.

Tien Pao grabbed Lieutenant Hamsun's arm. "My mother told me of this," he jabbered in excited Chinese. "At the great field for airplanes at Hengyang that I never saw. She said my father and the men were like goats of the mountains. She said my father and the men broke down the mountains with great dynamite blasts, and then they broke up the rocks from the blasts to make crushed stone for runways for the airplanes. And look! It is just what these men are doing. This isn't Hengyang, but, oh, my mother told me of this, and then she promised me that the next day I would go along to see it, too, but the river took me."

The mountain was gone, the plane was cruising along another part of the endless field. It dipped still lower, and now there were women working below—an endless file of women, each one with a carrying pole from which hung two baskets. They shuffled along in a single long file that reached from a hillside where men were scooping the baskets full of dirt. Then the never-ending, never-stopping file of women shuffled on again, and up a huge wall of dirt that the women were building up underneath themselves, basket by basket. It was like ants carrying grains of sand.

"They are building revetments for the bombers. That way they are protected from enemy air attack," the interpreter explained.

Tien Pao hardly heard, what he saw down below was too interesting and exciting. The walls of dirt that the women were building were in the shape of a U. The great mounds were open at only one end. The plane passed over a finished mound and in it stood a huge bomber plane, protected by dirt walls on three sides. They were like stables, Tien Pao thought—stables for bombers. They passed more finished revetments with bombers, but then again there was a row of partially finished mounds with women climbing up and down them with their little scoop baskets. A woman just emptying her baskets looked up as the low, roaring plane flew over.

Tien Pao screamed! "My mother! I saw my mother! My mother . . ."

Lieutenant Hamsun whipped around to him, startled. The interpreter stared down. But the plane flew on, the mound was gone. Tien Pao pummeled the lieutenant with hard, fierce fists. "My mother!" He pointed and pointed. "I saw my mother!"

Lieutenant Hamsun cast a startled look at the women down below, then at the interpreter. But he must somehow have understood what Tien Pao was screaming, and the interpreter forgot to translate. His eyes were searching along the revetments. "No, Tien Pao," Lieutenant Hamsun said. "You couldn't have seen your mother. There's hardly a chance."

It did not matter what the lieutenant said or in what language, Tien Pao did not hear him. The plane was going over buildings now. Never, never in all this enormous complicated field would they find that one revetment again. Tien Pao tried to keep the revetment in sight. He couldn't. It was gone. He sank down in a sobbing heap on the floor of the plane. He beat the floor with his hands. He had lost his mother. For a moment there she had been, but he had lost her.

"Tien Pao! Tien Pao! We'll go look. We'll go in for a landing, grab a jeep and race out there. . . . But you've got to understand—this isn't a wheelbarrow, I can't just let go of the handles and set it down. We're going in now, then we'll grab a jeep and find your revetment."

The lieutenant talked and talked, Tien Pao did not listen. Lieutenant Hamsun spoke impatient words to the interpreter, the interpreter hastily told Tien Pao what Lieutenant Hamsun had said. Tien Pao did not listen, he did not care what they said—he had seen his mother and he had lost her. Never, never in all this huge complicated field would they find that one particular revetment. Darkness would fall. The workers on the field would go home. . . .

The plane was down. Then Tien Pao and Lieutenant Hamsun, in spite of his bad leg, were running to a jeep standing beside a building. The interpreter came running behind—only he had remembered Glory-of-the-Republic. They jumped into the jeep without anybody's permission. Lieutenant Hamsun started the motor. A soldier came dashing out of the building, shouted at them, but Lieutenant Hamsun just shouted something over his shoulder and kept going.

Lieutenant Hamsun looked at Tien Pao and said things.

"The lieutenant says you mustn't build your hopes too high," the interpreter said weakly.

Tien Pao did not hear him; he stared straight ahead. Never in all this horrible long bouncing and weaving among all these drives and half-finished little roads would they find the revetment. Already Tien Pao was utterly confused, he hadn't the slightest idea which way they'd have to go. But then the jeep screeched around a short corner and they were on a wider road. They shot past built-up revetments that had bombers standing in them. They passed some low ones that were just going up. And then . . . and then the jeep roared right up to the high one on which his mother had been! Oh, Lieutenant Hamsun knew, he'd known all the time. He could see things from the air and know just where they were on the ground and how to get to them. Tien Pao could have bawled with relief. He jumped up in the moving jeep, and Lieutenant Hamsun hastily stopped it.

As they were getting out of the jeep, a bomber in

one of the great revetments across the road began a thundering roar. The wind from the huge propeller almost knocked Tien Pao against the jeep. It scared Glory-of-the-Republic so, he leaped from the interpreter's arms and bowled away as if blown by the terrific wind. The interpreter chased after him. Tien Pao did not wait, but raced up the mound of dirt past the row of shuffling women going down with their empty baskets. Lieutenant Hamsun came right behind him. And then Tien Pao stood in the exact spot where his mother had stood when she had looked up at the plane! He knew. He knew. Here she had stood and had looked up at him, but, of course, she didn't know.

With the lieutenant, Tien Pao examined each stooped woman as she trudged wearily up the mound with her loaded scoop baskets. They had their heads so bowed against the weight and the climb, it was hard to see their faces in the gathering evening dusk until they emptied the baskets. Lieutenant Hamsun stopped a woman who was emptying her basket at his toes. He stuffed some yen into her hand, then with an apologetic grin he pulled out his handkerchief and tied it to her yoke pole. He pointed it out to Tien Pao. "As if you wouldn't know your mother a mile off! But all Chinese look alike to me, and I've got to prove it to you if she isn't here. When at last this woman makes the circle you'll know we've seen them all. And oh, I dread seeing that moment come." Tien Pao did not seem aware that the lieutenant was talking, he kept searching the faces. Soon it would be dark, and they'd all go home. "Come soon now, Mother. Come soon." It kept saying itself over and over inside of him, as if it would hurry her on.

There were hundreds and hundreds of women, and always they came on, a few shuffling slow steps behind each other, backs bent, heads stooped, chins on chest. And then at last Lieutenant Hamsun saw the white handkerchief. Slowly it came up the line, slowly it climbed the mound. The lieutenant took Tien Pao's hand and held it tightly in his own.

Now the woman was emptying her basket right before Tien Pao's feet. But Tien Pao would not give up. He turned his back on her, and from the high mound searched the other revetments. The long night shadows were filtering down on the field, but still the work went on. At a sudden sound of singing, Tien Pao glanced down the field. And there came some hundred chanting women, pulling a huge stone roller that was crushing the fine rock into a hard road for a new runway. An overseer marched beside the mass of tugging women leaning in the ropes. He chanted, the women chanted back, and as they chanted they strained forward and tugged the roller ahead.

Tien Pao's hand jerked nervously in the lieutenant's grasp. Then with a loud, wild yell he jerked himself free, plunged down the revetment, plunged unseeing past the interpreter coming up with Glory-of-the-Republic, and tore madly across the crushed stone roadway straight at the roller. He plunged among the mass of tugging, chanting women. The roller stopped. There was an alarmed cackle of voices. The overseer barked loud, fierce words at the excited women, but the roller stood still. Tien Pao flung himself at a woman in the midst of the group. "MY MOTHER!"

The overseer ranted and shrieked. It made no matter. The women stood twisted in the ropes, they huddled around a kneeling, weeping woman who sobbed herself out against her son's chest. The women wept with her, laughed, asked bewildered questions that no one heard and no one answered.

Then Lieutenant Hamsun was there. He yelled something fierce at the ranting Chinese overseer, and behind him the interpreter with the little pig stopped to explain things to the overseer to calm him down. But Lieutenant Hamsun elbowed his way in among the women, waded into the heap of kneeling women. Tien Pao's mother, her eyes streaming, looked blindly up at him. "The father! The father!" she chattered wildly. "He is there on the mountain, he too must know it is Tien Pao."

"I'll go get the jeep," Lieutenant Hamsun shouted. Nobody heard him.

Tien Pao's mother wrenched herself out of the harness rope, grabbed Tien Pao's hand, and together they broke out of the heap of excited, chattering women. Tien Pao, not knowing what he was doing, pulled away from her, dashed to the interpreter, grabbed the little pig, and tore back to his mother. Together, hand in hand, they started running toward the distant, darkening mountain.

From far down the runway Lieutenant Hamsun shouted after them: "The jeep, the jeep! What's the jeep for? You can't run all that way. . . ."

They didn't hear him, and Lieutenant Hamsun turned and went on a limping run for the jeep. He forgot about the interpreter waiting near the roller, he forgot about roads and runways, he set out after Tien Pao and his mother across the rough field. He caught up with them. He almost had to lift Tien Pao's mother bodily into the jeep, she was too bewildered in her happy, delirious joy to be able to comprehend anything. The lieutenant set out for the mountain. He couldn't reach it. The strewn jagged rocks and enormous boulders hurled below the mountainside by dynamite blasts forced him to stop far from the foot of the dug-away mountain. But Tien Pao's mother jumped up in the jeep, and in the fierce strength of her joy she lifted Tien Pao high and screamed a terrible scream at the mountain. "It is Tien Pao! It is Tien Pao!"

Her cry rang up the mountainside. Men stopped

and looked down, and one man halfway up the rocky hill let his huge sledge hammer fall from his hand. He just stood. But then he bellowed it out: "It is Tien Pao!"

He came plunging down. He came straight down, straight toward the jeep. He used no paths. But he could not run that fast, not down a mountain. He fell. He struggled up again, and fell. He leaped up. All around him the men were shouting at him, running toward him. He half turned to them as he lunged on. "It is Tien Pao," he bellowed, and that answered all and explained all, and he came on in terrible, plunging strides.

Tien Pao's mother sank down on the seat, her strength suddenly all gone. Her whole body trembled, she clung fiercely to Tien Pao, and she cried. Softly she cried, and Tien Pao cried with her as they watched his plunging father. And in his happiness he had to tell Lieutenant Hamsun, who could not understand. "Oh, it was my mother, and I knew it. She had been on the revetment, but they called the younger women down to pull the roller to finish the job before dark. Oh, I knew it, I knew it. And my little sister is with neighbors in a little village near this airfield." Suddenly he remembered his little pig. He grabbed up Glory-of-the-Republic, he hugged him.

And as Tien Pao finished talking, his mother looked and looked her gratitude at the lieutenant. "It is Tien Pao," she softly told the lieutenant as if it were a wholly new and unbelievable thing. "It is Tien Pao." And in her gratitude this timid, shy Chinese woman leaned forward and laid her hand on the lieutenant's arm and talked to him in earnest Chinese, and the tears rolled unheeded down her cheeks.

"It is Tien Pao," she said again. "And tomorrow and tomorrow and tomorrow—and all the days to come—there will still be my little son. And the house won't be too empty and the anxious heart too full. . . . Ah, tomorrow, and tomorrow, and then will come a day when there will be no more shooting, and no more running from the shooting, and no war. There will come a day when the little family of Tien will go back to their little village, and live in peace. Ah, tomorrow and tomorrow. Ah, ah, ah."

She had no more words. She choked on them and her tears streamed. And there came his father, and his mother was clutching him fiercely again. There sat the lieutenant half turned, and he did not understand what his mother had said. Ah, but he did understand. He understood! The heart understands without words.

Set in Linotype Fairfield
Format by Terry Pace and Maurice Sendak
Lithographed by the Murray Printing Company
Published by HARPER & ROW, *Publishers*